STAR WARS®
A NEW HOPE: THE LIFE OF
LUKE SKYWALKER

Biographies
The Rise and Fall of Darth Vader
The Life and Legend of Obi-Wan Kenobi

Target
Hostage
Renegade
Firefight

STAR WARS®

A NEW HOPE: THE LIFE OF
LUKE SKYWALKER

BY RYDER WINDHAM

SCHOLASTIC INC.

New York   Toronto   London   Auckland   Sydney   Mexico City   New Delhi   Hong Kong

www.starwars.com
www.scholastic.com

ISBN-13: 978-0-545-09732-1
ISBN-10: 0-545-09732-0

12 11 10 9 8 7 6 5 4 3 2 1   9 10 11 12 13 14/0

Cover illustrations by Mike Butkus
Printed in the U.S.A.
First printing, September 2009

In memory of
Archie Goodwin

TABLE OF CONTENTS

STAR WARS®

A NEW HOPE: THE LIFE OF
LUKE SKYWALKER

PROLOGUE

"*Do you ever wonder about our father, Leia?*"
Luke asked.

"*No,*" Leia said without hesitation. "*I never do.*"

*Luke Skywalker and Princess Leia Organa were
on board the* New Hope, *a Dreadnaught-class heavy
cruiser that currently served as the flagship for Mon
Mothma, the recently elected chief councilor of the
fledgling New Republic. They were in a meeting room
near the cruiser's command deck, standing before a
wide viewport that overlooked a small red planet orbiting a bright sun.*

"*Oh,*" Luke said. "*I don't know how to say this,
but . . . well, it's been months since he died, and I think
there are some things we should talk about. I know
you're still upset about how he —*"

"*Tortured me?*" Leia interrupted. "*Stood by and
did nothing while Grand Moff Tarkin destroyed the
planet Alderaan? Cut off your hand? Killed more*

1

people than we'll ever know?" She gestured to the red planet outside the viewport and added, "Do you have any idea how many Chubbits died on Aridus because of Vader?"

Luke knew a great deal about the unfortunate Chubbits, but he remained silent.

As Leia gazed into space, she said, "It seems everywhere we go, we find more of Vader's victims, more evidence of his horrific service to the Empire." She shook her head. "Why would I even want to think about that monster?"

"Because our father wasn't just Darth Vader," Luke said. "He was also Anakin Skywalker, a Jedi. I've tried to tell you what happened on the Death Star at Endor, how he saved me from the Emperor and —"

"Saved you?" Leia said. "Luke, as I recall, Vader delivered you to the Emperor." She sighed. "I know you believe that Anakin Skywalker returned in the end, and if that's how you prefer to remember him, as the Jedi hero who destroyed the Emperor, that's your decision. But you can't expect me to do the same, because my father, Bail Organa, the man who raised me, he died on Alderaan."

"I'm sorry, Leia," Luke said. "I just thought —"

"You thought wrong, Luke," Leia said. "I have more important things on my mind than this. In case you haven't noticed, the Empire didn't die with the Emperor. We don't know how many Star Destroyers are still in service. *Moff Harlov Jarnek has blockaded Spirador. Hundreds of planets still need our help."* She moved away from the viewport. *"Now, if you'll excuse me, I have a meeting to attend. The Chubbits are justifiably cautious of offworlders, but I'm determined to convince them that an alliance with the New Republic is their best defense against the Empire."* She turned and walked for the meeting room's exit.

Alone in the room, Luke returned his gaze to Aridus. He'd visited the desert planet before. Except that it had a single sun, he'd found it very similar to his own homeworld, Tatooine.

So much had happened since the day he'd left Mos Eisley Spaceport with Ben Kenobi on the Millennium Falcon. Back then, his greatest desire had been to have adventures on other worlds. He'd never imagined that he would eventually encounter the father he'd been told was dead, discover that Princess Leia was his sister, or become a champion of the Rebel Alliance.

But despite his accomplishments and many good friends, Luke sensed there was something missing in his life, as if part of him were somehow incomplete. The Empire had destroyed nearly all the records of the Jedi Order, including any information about Anakin Skywalker, leaving Luke with many questions about his place in the universe.

Can I avoid my father's mistakes?

Are all the other Jedi Knights truly gone?

How can I be a good Jedi when I know so little about them?

Despite Leia's apparent lack of interest, Luke believed it was important for him to find out more about the life of Anakin Skywalker.

How can I know myself if I never really knew my father?

He had no idea whether gaining such knowledge would make him feel wiser or more fulfilled. All he knew was that he still felt alone and out of place, just as he'd felt when he was a little boy, growing up on a desolate moisture farm in the desert wastes of Tatooine. . . .

CHAPTER ONE

"Is someone seeing me, Aunt Beru?" Luke asked.

Beru Lars was standing in her kitchen, making biscuits. She glanced at the four-year-old boy, her husband's stepbrother's son, who sat on the hard white steps that led up to the dining alcove, and said, "Your aunt Dama will be seeing all of us. She should be here any time now."

Luke frowned. "No. I don't mean Aunt Dama. I mean, is someone *watching* me?"

Beru smiled. "You're right here with me, so I'm watching you."

The boy shook his head. "No. Not you or Uncle Owen. I mean someone else. Someone I can't see."

Beru almost dropped the spoon she had just picked up. She set the spoon down beside a bowl with a gray mixture in it and tried to keep her voice calm as she asked, "What makes you say that, Luke?"

Luke was holding a small toy landspeeder. As he turned the toy over in his hands, he said, "I just felt like someone else was close by. I thought maybe there was somebody behind me, but when I looked up the steps . . ." He turned his head to look back toward the dining alcove, then returned his gaze to his aunt. "No one's there."

Beru sighed. "Living far from other folks like we do, it's not unusual to get a bit jumpy. You feel a small shift in the air, or hear a slight noise, and your imagination starts playing tricks on you."

"Really?" Luke said. "But I didn't hear the wind or anything this time."

Beru gripped the edge of the kitchen counter to steady herself. She said, "There's been *other* times you thought someone else was watching?"

"Sometimes when I play outside," Luke said. "And every time we go into Anchorhead."

Beru stepped away from the counter to kneel down beside Luke. Gripping his upper arms gently, she said, "Luke, this is important. You've never, ever actually seen any man watching you, have you?"

Luke cocked his head sideways as he held his aunt's gaze. "You think it's a man?"

Beru shook her head. "No, sorry, I didn't mean to say that. I meant any*one,* any *person.* You've never noticed anyone?"

Luke shook his head. "No, ma'am."

Just then they heard the sound of a landspeeder engine drift down outside, and Uncle Owen bellowed, "Beru! Your sister's here!"

Beru's eyes flicked to the dining cove, then back to Luke. She said, "I think it's best that we don't mention any of this to your uncle. This feeling you get some-times, it might worry him. You know how he is about strangers and trespassers. And we don't want to worry Uncle Owen, do we?"

"No, ma'am," Luke said. "So, it's only a feeling? There's no one really watching me?"

"That's right," Beru said. "Now, come on, let's go greet your aunt Dama."

Luke got up, clutching his toy landspeeder in his hand.

The Lars homestead on Tatooine consisted of vari-ous underground rooms that branched off a deep, steep-walled open pit that was the central courtyard. Beru took Luke's free hand and led him out across the courtyard, up a flight of steps along the pit's wall, and then up through an enclosed stairway. It was a long climb for a little boy, but Luke didn't complain. He said, "Aunt Dama has a new landspeeder."

"How do you know that?" Beru asked.

"Before Uncle Owen called you, I heard the engine coming. It sounds less rumbly than the old one."

The enclosed stairway delivered them to the arched doorway of the homestead's pourstone entry dome. As

Luke and Beru stepped out through the doorway and into the blazing heat of Tatooine's twin suns, a smiling, round-faced woman walked up to them and said, "There you are!"

"Hi, Aunt Dama," Luke said. He held out his toy. "I have a landspeeder too!"

Dama Whitesun Brunk was Beru's younger sister. Like Owen, Dama's husband, Sam, was a moisture farmer. They lived in Anchorhead, one of Tatooine's oldest settlements, where they owned and operated a small hotel. Although Anchorhead was only twenty kilometers away from the Lars homestead, Dama and Sam seldom visited.

"My, my, Luke," Dama said as she bent down to give Luke a hug. "You're growing faster than a ronto!" Releasing Luke, she stood up and embraced her sister. "I'm so happy to see you, Beru."

"You look well, Dama."

"Sorry we haven't visited you in so long. Between managing the farm and the hotel, seems like we're always busy."

Luke looked past Dama to see Sam Brunk and Uncle Owen standing beside a dark green landspeeder with a bubble canopy and three sleek thrusters on each side. Wanting a closer look at the vehicle, he began walking toward it. Owen and Sam were facing away from him, gazing at the tall moisture vaporator units that were neatly spaced away from each other across the

surrounding salt flat, and talking about what most moisture farmers usually talked about.

"How's your crop?"

"Can't complain."

"I had to replace two vaporators."

"Broken?"

"Stolen."

"Jawas?"

"Probably."

Seeing that the two men were still so engaged in
their conversation that they hadn't noticed him, Luke
moved up close beside the parked speeder and studied
the emblem and Aurebesh lettering that were posi-
tioned below the canopy's rim: *Mobquet A-1 Deluxe
Floater*. He was proud that he'd learned how to read
Basic from a set of old educational datatapes that Aunt
Beru had given him, but wasn't sure how to pronounce
Mobquet.

Luke moved around to the front of the speeder and
was admiring the design of the inlet ports that ringed its
rounded nose when he noticed Beru and Dama walking
over toward their husbands. Dama rolled her eyes and
said, "I suppose you two are talking about Tatooine's
rich, cultural history again?"

Sam Brunk chuckled, then said, "No, but speaking
of history . . . did you hear that the Empire outlawed
Podracing?"

Beru and Owen shook their heads.

Sam continued, "Heard it on a HoloNet report. At first, I figured the Empire would affect Tatooine about as much as the Republic did, which was not at all. But there's already talk that the Mos Espa Arena might be shuttin' down. If that happens, there'll be no more Podraces for. . . ." Sam's gaze had drifted to an area beyond the homestead's open pit. "Say, something's different over there."

Beru said, "Where?"

"There," Sam said, pointing. "Didn't you have some supply tanks, or some kind of . . . ?" Sam stopped talking, and then everyone was silent.

Luke noticed the sudden quiet and turned his head to follow the adults' gaze to the southwest. Except for some moisture vaporators in the distance, there was nothing to see but scorched ground.

"Sorry, Owen," Sam said, finally breaking the awkward silence. "I just realized what was, uh, missing. It's the headstones."

Owen said nothing, but just kept his eyes to the southwest.

Sam said, "I, uh, hope it wasn't vandals. . . ."

"No," Owen said. "I removed the headstones."

"Oh," Sam said.

Without any further explanation, Owen turned and headed for the entry dome. After he was gone, Beru said, "Please forgive Owen. He . . . he just didn't see a need for anyone to know where Shmi was buried."

"But he removed *all* the headstones," Sam said. "His parents and uncle were buried there too, yes?"

Beru nodded.

Luke said, "Who's Shmi?"

Beru jumped. She hadn't seen Luke in front of the parked speeder and didn't know that he'd been listening. She glanced at Dama, then back at Luke and said, "Shmi was your grandmother, Luke."

"Oh," he said. "Is my father buried there too?"

"No," Beru said. "Your father didn't die on Tatooine."

"Oh," he said again. Then he looked at Dama and Sam and said, "My father was a navigator on a spice freighter. Uncle Owen told me so."

CHAPTER TWO

It had been a long time since Luke Skywalker had felt like someone was watching him. A few years, at least. But he felt it now.

He jumped to his feet and looked around. He'd been lying on a blanket that he'd stretched out on the sand so he could be comfortable while he gazed at the night sky. Now he was anything but relaxed.

He glanced back in the direction of his home. He half expected to see his uncle trudging toward him, but there was no sign of movement between his position and the winking lights on the distant security sensors that ringed the moisture farm's perimeter.

Like any seven-year-old child on Tatooine, Luke knew the dangers of straying too far from home at any time of day, let alone the middle of the night. Hidden sinkholes and sudden sandstorms were deadly threats, as were various nasty creatures always looking for a meal. Womp rats traveled in packs and had claws and teeth that could easily slice through flesh. Hulking krayt dragons roamed the mountains and canyons of the Jundland Wastes. Worst of all were the Sand People, the masked nomads also known as Tusken Raiders, who sometimes attacked and killed without any obvious motive or reason. More than once, Luke had heard his uncle say, "If the heat doesn't kill you on Tatooine, everything else will."

Luke recalled other times when he'd had the sensation of being watched by some invisible presence. His aunt Beru knew about at least one time, when he was four, because he'd told her. What he didn't tell her, because he didn't know how to explain it and didn't want to hurt her feelings, was that he had taken some comfort in the idea of someone else watching over him. But then she'd told him his mind had just been playing tricks on him, or something like that, and he'd stopped thinking about it.

Luke scanned the dark horizon. Still no sign of movement. The only sound he heard was the pounding of his own heart. He tried to convince himself that he hadn't really been frightened, and that he was merely nervous with excitement. He took a deep breath to calm down, and, as he did so, he knew he had overreacted. He was certain that no one was watching him. He knew he was alone.

All alone.

Still standing, he tilted his head back to look at the stars that filled the sky. He'd memorized the names of many worlds and stellar bodies in the Arkanis Sector, the region of space in the galaxy's Outer Rim, which included Tatooine's binary star system. There was Arkanis which boasted a starship pilot training facility. Both Andooweel and C-Foroon were said to be refuges for smugglers and pirates, as was the water planet Tarnoonga. He knew little about Najiba, Tythe, Hypori, or Siskeen but had heard that Geonosis had been the location of the first battle of the Clone Wars, the great interstellar conflict which had ended shortly after he was born. Luke suspected that all these worlds were far more interesting than Tatooine.

A bright flare streaked across the northern hemisphere before it vanished. Luke smiled as he held his breath and waited. A moment later, two more streaks radiated from the same direction. Luke had heard some folks call such streaks of light "shooting stars," and his uncle often said, "People can believe what they like." But Luke knew that the streaks were meteors, bits of debris striking and burning up in Tatooine's atmosphere, and he maintained that anyone who called them shooting stars was just plain wrong.

Out of the corner of his eye, he noticed a bright point of light that appeared to be moving slowly, drifting up from the northern horizon. He realized at once that it was a spacecraft, reflecting the light from Tatooine's suns. From its trajectory, he guessed it had launched from Mos Eisley Spaceport, roughly fifty kilometers away. He wondered if it might be a spice freighter. For all he knew, he was looking at the same ship that had once carried his father.

Luke watched the moving point of light until it vanished into space. He wondered if the ship might leave the Arkanis Sector. He could only imagine where the ship was headed, but he wished he were on it anyway.

He stooped down to pick up the blanket and the small container of water he'd brought with him and began walking home. He paused twice to look at the stars again, and it took him almost twenty minutes to reach the security sensors.

He dipped his hand into a pocket and withdrew a droid caller he'd rigged to allow him to sneak past the small, roving guard droids that patrolled the homestead's perimeter. Out of habit, he walked carefully around the area where he knew the bodies of his grandmother and Owen's parents and uncle were buried.

Luke still knew precious little about his own family, because Owen barely spoke at all about them. At some point, Luke had learned that Owen's uncle was named Edern, and that he'd died at the age of fourteen when he lost control of a landspeeder. As for any information about Luke's mother, both Owen and Beru claimed that they knew nothing about her.

Carrying the rigged droid caller and thinking of the dead, Luke was only a few steps from the entry dome when his uncle appeared unexpectedly in the dome's arched doorway. Owen was carrying a long laser rifle. Luke was alarmed to find himself staring straight down the weapon's barrel.

Owen jumped when he saw Luke, jerking the rifle back sharply to raise its barrel to the sky. Luke stood frozen in his tracks.

Owen scowled. "I was coming to look for you," he said. "Just two minutes ago, your aunt went to check in on you. Found your loft empty." He shook his head. "Boy, what were you doing out there? Trying to get yourself killed?"

"No, sir," Luke said. The blanket he carried suddenly felt very heavy.

"Well, what, then?"

"I'm sorry," Luke said. "I heard some kids at Anchorhead say there'd be a meteor shower, and I just wanted a clear view. I know you don't like to turn off the lights around here, but they make it hard to see the sky at night."

Owen's face went red. "You risked your neck to see a meteor shower?"

"I missed the last one," Luke said. "They don't happen that often. I'm sorry, sir. I didn't mean to make you angry. I just wanted to —"

"Inside," Owen said. "Now. And straight to bed."
As Luke moved past him, Owen added, "Hang on. Hand over that droid caller."

Luke gave the device to him.

"We'll talk about this in the morning."

"Yes, sir."

As Luke lay on the mat in his sleeping loft, he couldn't help overhearing his uncle and aunt's heated discussion through the air vent that overlooked the central courtyard.

Owen said, "I'm telling you, I'm really at my wit's end with that boy."

"You know he didn't mean to upset us."

"That's not the point, Beru. He can't go wandering off as he pleases."

"Did you always do everything your father told you to do?"

"This has nothing to do with my father."

"I know. I just meant that boys don't always listen to —"

"Oh, come now, you can't be taking Luke's side in this. Tell me, honestly, what if something had happened to him out there? And . . . and what if I'd gone looking for him, and I'd walked straight into a bunch of Tuskens? Would *that* have convinced you . . ."

"Owen, please, keep your voice down."

". . . that maybe I have a good reason to worry about whether Luke does as I say? Honestly, Beru, I don't enjoy bossing him around. But if he won't listen to us, what's going to happen to him?"

"Maybe he'd listen to someone else. Maybe Ob —"

"Hush! You keep that man's name out of our home."

Luke held his breath as he listened. He had no idea who his aunt and uncle were talking about, but he'd never heard his uncle snap at his aunt like that.

"Well, Owen," Beru continued, "if, like you say, you're at your wit's end, what do you propose to do about it?"

"Well, I think it's best to keep the boy occupied. Maybe he needs some more chores."

Hearing this, Luke almost groaned out loud, but he stayed silent.

"More chores?" Beru laughed. "What more can he do? Owen, he's only seven years old."

"He needs to understand the importance of personal responsibility."

"Luke already runs himself ragged for you."

"Not ragged enough, apparently, if he has the energy to sneak off in the middle of the night. And on Tatooine! Isn't that boy afraid of anything?"

"Oh, listen to yourself," Beru said. "Would it make you happier if he were afraid of you?"

"No, of course not," Owen said. "It's just that . . . when I stepped out to look for him tonight, I was carrying my laser rifle, and . . . Beru, I was startled. If I hadn't set the rifle's safety switch . . ."

"Oh, Owen!"

". . . I might have shot him."

"Well, thank goodness you set the safety."

There was silence for a moment. Then Owen said, "Living here, surviving here, it helps if you have some degree of fear so you can be careful and stay alive. I'm not doing a very good job of raising Luke if I can't convince him he should be afraid of Tuskens."

"Maybe that shouldn't surprise us," Beru said. "His father wasn't afraid of Tuskens either."

Luke's eyes widened at the mention of his father. He listened carefully, waiting for more details. Instead, there was another brief silence before Owen said, "Let's not get into that. It's been a long day. We both need to get some rest."

Luke stared at the ceiling for a long time, thinking of the father he would never know, until he finally drifted off to sleep.

The next morning, Luke went to the dining alcove for breakfast. He wasn't looking forward to facing his uncle, as he expected a long lecture about responsibility and all the dangers he'd already heard about before. He found his uncle seated at the dining table, finishing the last bits of food on the plate in front of him. Beru stepped up from the kitchen, carrying a plate of food for Luke, and she smiled as she saw him approach.

"Good morning," Luke said as he took his seat.

Beru set down Luke's plate in front of him. As she picked up Owen's empty plate, Owen lifted his gaze to meet Luke's eyes.

Luke felt his face flush. "I'm really sorry about last night, Uncle Owen. I . . . I never meant to make you angry, and I promise I'll —"

Owen raised a hand and shook his head slightly, signaling Luke to stop. "Let's hold off on promises," he said, "because they can be hard to keep."

Uh-oh, Luke thought. *Here comes the lecture.*

Beru said, "I'll let you two talk alone." She turned and descended to the kitchen.

Owen shifted his elbows on the table. "Luke, I've been accused of worrying too much about the people I care about, and I won't deny it. And I know from experience that a man can't take care of everything. Things happen. Sometimes people leave, and you think they'll be comin' back, but they don't. Do you understand?"

Luke wasn't sure, but he nodded.

"Well, I can't protect you all the time," Owen continued, "and I certainly can't teach you to be as cautious as I am. But after doing some thinking, I've come up with a solution that might at least make me worry less. I should warn you, though, I already told your aunt about this solution, and she doesn't like it one bit."

Luke braced himself. He was certain that his uncle was about to ground him or give him more chores. Or both.

Owen took a sip from a water cup, then said, "I was just about your age when my father taught me how to handle a laser rifle. I do believe I'd worry a bit less about you if you knew how to handle one too."

Luke's mouth fell open. "A laser rifle? Really?"

"You can have my uncle's old one. It's still good. After breakfast, we'll go over some safety basics, then do a little target practice."

"Wow!" Luke said. "Thanks, Uncle Owen!"

"You can thank me by living a good, long life," Owen replied. Then he leveled a finger at Luke and said, "And if you ever wander off on your own again, don't you even *think* of leaving without a weapon."

"Yes, sir."

"I'll go get the rifle," Owen said, rising from the table. "Now eat up before your food gets cold."

Owen left the alcove. Luke gobbled down his breakfast, then carried his plate and utensils to the kitchen, where he found his aunt canning vegetables. She looked up at him. "I don't have to tell you to be careful out there, do I?"

"No, ma'am." He was about to leave when he stopped, turned to Beru, and said, "When my father left, did he tell Uncle Owen that he was gonna come back?"

Beru frowned slightly, then said, "Oh, Luke. You know it's best not to wonder about such things."

"But did he?"

She shook her head. "No," she said. "He didn't. He didn't say anything. He . . . he just left."

Luke bit his lower lip, then said, "I'd never do that. Leave without saying good-bye, I mean."

Beru smiled. "I know you wouldn't." She stepped over and gave Luke a hug.

"Gosh, you're squeezin' me," Luke said, laughing. Beru released him and he said, "See you later." He ran up the steps, eager to catch up with his uncle.

CHAPTER THREE

By the age of thirteen, Luke was a crack shot with his laser rifle, which certainly encouraged womp rats to keep their distance from the Lars homestead. He also knew just about everything there was to know about maintaining moisture vaporators, and he had a good deal of experience refurbishing Treadwell droids. His technical skills encouraged his uncle to allow him to work on the family landspeeder, a black SoroSuub V-35 Courier.

But because he had no genuine interest in pest control, moisture farming, or fixing Treadwells, and because it would be a cold day on Tatooine before Owen would let a thirteen-year-old boy drive a landspeeder, Luke found himself growing increasingly restless for any kind of diversion. As much as he loved his aunt and uncle, he didn't believe that he could ever understand them.

Living on a desert world in the Outer Rim was their choice, he thought. *Not mine.*

He wasn't completely isolated. He had a small computer that he usually kept in his sleeping loft, and he sometimes used it to communicate with other kids, including his best friend, Biggs Darklighter. Biggs lived on his father's moisture farm just eight kilometers away, which made them practically neighbors. He was five years older than Luke, but they shared common interests in high-speed repulsorlift vehicles and interstellar travel. Biggs also had no desire to become a moisture farmer, and he talked often of his plans to leave Tatooine and go to the Academy.

One evening, after dinner, Luke brought his computer into the tech dome, the underground family garage, so he could view instructions for assembling a scale model of a T-16 skyhopper. He had the model's pieces laid out on his workbench and was about to secure a stabilizer into place when his computer made a beeping sound. Luke knew that Biggs had gone with his family to Mos Espa, and hoped the incoming call was from him.

He pressed a button and watched the skyhopper instructions vanish from the computer's oval monitor, which then displayed a flickering image of a dark-haired boy. It was Windy Starkiller, who was also thirteen and lived on a nearby moisture farm with his parents.

"Hey, Windy," Luke said.

"Luke, I just got home from Anchorhead with my folks. Wanna know what Fixer and Tank called us?"

"Huh?"

"They called us small fry. Can you believe that?"

"Small fry?"

"Yeah, just because we're not old enough to drive landspeeders and they are. They were bragging about going racing in the canyon south of Ja-Mero Ridge tomorrow afternoon. They said it was 'more than small fry like you and Skywalker could ever handle.' What a couple of jerks."

Luke winced. "They called us jerks too?"

"Not us, you idiot," Windy said, rolling his eyes. "Them! They're the jerks!"

"Oh," Luke said. He didn't want Windy to know that he felt hurt by what the other boys had said. Fixer, whose real name was Laze Loneozner, was always trying to repair one thing or another, and Janek Sunber was called Tank because he was bigger than the other kids. They practically lived at Tosche Station, the power station outside Anchorhead, and Luke liked them both. Or *had* liked them. He'd thought they were his friends.

"We oughtta do something," Windy said. "Something to prove we're not small fry! Something . . . I dunno . . . dangerous!"

Luke pursed his lips, then said, "How's Huey?"

"Fine," Windy said. "Why?"

"Bring him over tomorrow morning," Luke said. "We'll take him for a ride."

25

"Where?"

"I'll tell you tomorrow. Oh, and bring your rifle." Luke broke the connection and Windy's image flickered off the computer screen.

Huey was a young dewback, a four-legged, green-skinned lizard. He was not fully grown, but was large and strong enough to carry two people at once. Although he mostly resided on Windy's family's property, Luke had helped raise Huey from a pup, and the two boys considered him their shared pet.

Luke was waiting for Windy and Huey when they arrived early at the Lars homestead. He had already checked and rechecked the items on his utility belt and cleaned the sand goggles that dangled from a strap around his neck. He held his laser rifle away from his body, its barrel aimed at the bright blue sky, just as Owen had taught him.

Windy straddled the saddle on Huey's broad back, which also carried Windy's rifle and various provisions. When Huey saw Luke, he trotted faster across the salt flat until he came to a quick stop in front of Luke, then bumped his green snout affectionately against Luke's chest.

Windy said, "Where's your uncle?"

"Out on the south range," Luke said as he gave Huey a pat. "Did you bring your scanner to check the weather?"

Windy patted the large leather pouch at the side of his utility belt and said, "Wouldn't leave home without it. Got my comlink too."

Luke secured his own rifle, then climbed up onto the saddle so he sat in front of Windy. Grabbing the reins, he glanced back at Windy and said, "All set?"

"You still haven't told me where we're going."

"Ja-Mero Ridge."

Windy gasped. "Are you crazy? That's in the Jundland Wastes!"

"You *said* we should do something dangerous. And just think . . . when Fixer and Tank go racing this afternoon, imagine the looks on their faces when they find us way out there, shooting womp rats. Bet they never traveled *that* far on their own before they got their landspeeders!"

"I dunno," Windy said. "It'll take us hours to get there."

"Huey can handle it," Luke said. "Besides, he needs the exercise. And we don't want anyone calling us small fry, right?"

"Yeah," Windy said, quickly warming to the idea. "You're right. Fixer and Tank will be speechless when they see us. Let's go!"

Luke gave the reins a tug as he pressed his ankles gently against Huey's sides. Huey turned and trotted away from the Lars homestead, carrying the boys toward the Jundland Wastes.

Luke smiled. It was a beautiful day. There wasn't a cloud in the sky.

"I thought you checked the weather before we left, Windy!" Luke shouted over the roaring wind as he guided Huey toward a cluster of towering buttes.

"Relax, Skywalker!" Windy shouted back. "It didn't say anything about a sandswirl!"

"Well, Huey's getting restless!"

Huey responded with a nervous grunt as he lowered his head and trotted faster.

High winds tore at the two boys and their dewback mount. They'd been traveling for far more hours than they'd anticipated along the edge of the Jundland Wastes, keeping a careful watch for Tusken Raiders and other predators. They had pretended not to notice the sky that began to darken as evening fell, but could not ignore the winds that had blown in as if from nowhere. They knew that a storm was coming and that they couldn't stay out in the open. To make matters worse, Windy had just discovered that he'd accidentally overcharged his comlink's battery, leaving them without any way to summon help.

Luke had studied an old datatape at home when he'd plotted their journey to Ja-Mero Ridge, and he thought he'd found a shortcut. But as they approached one butte that was bracketed by two others, he suddenly realized he wasn't sure which way to go.

Luke said, "I say we take the right fork."

"Left!" Windy said. "It's to the left!"

Huey grunted again. Holding tight to the reins, Luke guided the dewback to the right, and the boys found themselves moving past two walls of rock. As the space between the walls narrowed, Luke noticed an unusual stillness in the air. He said in a low whisper, "I got a bad feeling about this."

They emerged from the passage onto a high ledge that hugged the edge of the butte. The ledge overlooked the twisted canyons of the Jundland Wastes, and Tatooine's two suns hung low on the horizon. Massive storm clouds loomed in the bloodred sky above the Wastes. The clouds appeared to be growing and expanding, moving toward the boys' position with the all the subtlety of an enormous malevolent beast.

The wind picked up suddenly. Luke knew they needed to find shelter fast. He dug his ankles into Huey's side, and the dewback bolted forward along the ledge, which descended into a steep incline. Windy clung to the grips on the side of the saddle as Huey galloped down the incline that wrapped around the butte.

The wind was howling and Huey was still running fast when they arrived at the base of the canyon. Huey was in midrun when he let out a whining snort, as if he'd gotten a whiff of something he didn't like, and then he stopped and reared without warning.

Luke and Windy were thrown from Huey's back. Windy screamed as they tumbled to the hard ground.

Luke pushed himself up in time to see the frightened dewback race into a dark, narrow-walled ravine, taking the rifles and provisions with him.

Luke reached out to help Windy get up, but Windy shoved his hand aside and shouted, "All this is your fault! It was your idea to come out here!"

"Well, you fried the comlink!" Luke said. Furious, he pulled a strip of cloth from a pouch on his utility belt and wrapped it around the lower half of his face.

Ducking into a wall's shallow alcove, Windy tried to escape the stinging bits of fine sand that whipped through the canyon. Seeing Luke securing the cloth strip over his face, he said, "What do you think you're doing, Skywalker?"

"I'm going to find Huey," Luke said as he pulled his goggles up over his eyes. "His homing instinct is the only thing that can get us home."

"You'll never make it! You'll never find your way back!"

"Huey can't be too far," Luke said. He started to walk off.

Windy watched Luke for a moment, then said, "I'm not staying in here by myself!" He pulled on his own goggles as he moved after Luke.

They entered the ravine and began calling for Huey. The dewback responded immediately with two urgent grunts. They found him hugging the ground and trembling with fear a short distance away. The rifles and other gear were still strapped across his back.

"It's okay, little guy," Luke said as he placed his hands on Huey's head, trying to comfort him. "We'll get you to cover."

Luke looked at Windy and saw him standing rigid beside Huey. Windy was stammering Luke's name as he pointed down the length of the ravine. Luke followed Windy's gaze to see an immense shadowy form shift amid the swirling dust and sand.

It was a krayt dragon.

Luke gasped. The monster's wide, massive body very nearly filled the ravine. It lumbered forward, brushing against the rocky walls as it raised its horned head to display a mouth filled with thick, sharp fangs.

Luke knew if he didn't do something fast, he'd be dead. He jumped behind Huey and practically pounced on his laser rifle. He yanked the rifle free, swung the stock up against the right side of his chest, aimed for the krayt's head, and fired two quick bursts.

The krayt stopped and jerked its head back as the fired energy bolts slammed into it, right between the eyes. Seeing that he'd slowed the krayt, Luke clutched his rifle with his right hand while he reached out with his left to pull Windy's rifle free. "Come on, Windy!" Luke said as he held the other rifle out to his friend.

But Windy didn't take the offered weapon. Instead, he said, "Run, Luke! Run!"

"No!" Luke said. "We can hold him off!"

Windy panicked. He turned fast, knocking his own rifle from Luke's hand before he started running back the way they'd come.

The krayt roared. Luke raised his rifle and squeezed off more energy bolts into the krayt's head. As the krayt roared again and advanced in his direction, Luke realized that he'd only managed to make the monster more enraged.

The krayt lunged at Luke. Huey made a sudden jerk that knocked Luke aside, throwing him back after Windy's fleeing form. Luke rolled across the hard ground. As he raised his gaze back to the krayt, he heard a terrible crunching sound and saw the krayt biting down on Huey.

No!

Huey's body went limp and dangled from the krayt's jaws. Luke backed away slowly, slinking after Windy and hoping the krayt wouldn't notice his movement. Before he rounded a turn in the ravine, he glanced back at Huey and whimpered, "I'm sorry."

He tried to ignore the sound of the krayt tearing into the dewback.

As the ravine grew darker, Luke realized that the suns had finally set. He took a glowlamp from his belt and activated it so he could see better, but moved carefully so he wouldn't cast any shadows that might attract the krayt.

He heard Windy sobbing and felt a rush of anger. If he could hear Windy's sobs, he guessed the krayt might hear them too. He arrived outside the mouth of a shallow, low-ceilinged cave. He held the glowlamp before him as he entered the cave, and saw Windy slumped against the wall with his hands over his face.

"It's coming for us," Windy cried. "We're dead."

Luke heard a loud shuffling sound from outside the cave. He whispered, "Windy, be quiet."

Windy sobbed. "Mama . . . Mama . . ."

A moment later, there was a tremendous crash as the krayt's horned head slammed against the mouth of the cave. Because of Windy's sobbing, Luke had not heard the krayt's approach. Luke and Windy fell back to the deepest recess as the krayt drew back. Then the krayt launched itself again at the cave's entrance, ramming it so hard that it shattered rock.

Windy screamed, "We're dead!"

As the krayt prepared to throw its full weight against the crumbling wall, a strange, eerie howl drifted through the ravine and echoed off its walls.

Luke said, "What's that sound?"

Windy held his breath for a moment, then replied, "The wind?"

The howl continued for a moment longer, then died off. Luke peered cautiously out of the cave and saw the krayt lying on the ground. Its eyes were closed, and it was making a rumbling sound through its flared nostrils. Luke realized that it had fallen asleep.

Luke thought he saw a figure move in the darkness beyond the krayt's slumbering form. He held very still and watched the area for several seconds but decided he must have just seen some dust shifting in the ravine. The krayt remained motionless.

Turning back to Windy, Luke said, "It's asleep. We can get past it."

"And go where?" Windy said, outraged. "Without Huey? In the middle of a sandswirl? We're *never* going to find the way home." He shook his head and began to sob again. "They'll find our bones one day. Just old bones."

Luke was about to grab Windy and haul him out of the cave when he heard a man clearing his throat. Both boys turned their heads fast to see a hooded figure standing outside the cave. He was wearing a dark brown robe and holding a staff that was topped by a slender glow-rod. The figure pulled back his hood to reveal the weathered face of a white-haired, bearded man.

"I'm Ben Kenobi," the man said. "We don't have much time if I'm going to get you boys home."

INTERLUDE

Still on board the New Hope *in orbit of Aridus, Luke recalled how Ben Kenobi had taken him and Windy back to the Lars homestead. Luke's uncle and aunt had been waiting with Windy's parents, who were extremely grateful to Ben for rescuing their son. Everyone was stunned when Owen abruptly told Ben to leave and not to come back.*

The experience had left Luke baffled. Even now, some ten years after the incident, he still did not know why Owen had been so angry with Ben. From what little he knew, he assumed that Ben's purpose on Tatooine had been to discreetly watch over him while Owen and Beru raised him as if he were an ordinary child, not the son of a Jedi-turned-Sith Lord. But if both Ben and Owen had been responsible for protecting Luke, why hadn't they gotten along? Luke could only imagine why Owen had so aggressively objected to Ben's presence.

Luke remembered listening to conversations between his uncle and aunt, practically spying on them, hoping to hear any small detail about his father or Ben Kenobi. Owen and Beru never revealed much but merely reinforced that they preferred not to discuss either man.

Once, when Luke was about seventeen, Owen had become outraged when Beru had mentioned Anakin in front of Luke. After Owen had stormed off, Luke had asked his aunt what had happened between his father and Owen. His aunt had fumbled with words, said something about how Owen might have been disappointed when Luke's father had chosen to leave Tatooine, and without even saying good-bye. Luke couldn't recall exactly what Beru had said, but suspected she hadn't been entirely truthful, possibly to protect him from any knowledge of Darth Vader. He was left to wonder how well his uncle and aunt had known Anakin, and whether they had ever even liked him.

It suddenly occurred to Luke . . . If they did know my father, maybe they were afraid of him because he was fearless?

Often Uncle Owen had often reprimanded Luke for lacking fear. Luke had never felt especially courageous, just restless for adventure, ever ready to seize an opportunity to journey beyond the limited range of the Lars homestead. If he'd ever been afraid of anything, it was that he might wind up stuck on the sand planet forever.

Still, he could now understand why his uncle had been so frustrated with him, a boy who so often seemed to lack common sense as well as fear. He wondered what Owen would have thought if he'd known about the first time Luke had been truly terrified. . . .

CHAPTER FOUR

"Don't be scared," Biggs Darklighter said. "Climb in."

"Who're you calling scared?" Luke said as he secured his laser rifle next to Biggs's weapon on the back of his friend's landspeeder, which was parked a short distance from the entry dome to Luke's home. "Just because you're five years older'n me doesn't make you five years braver!"

It was Luke's fifteenth year on Tatooine, and he desperately wished he had his own landspeeder. His uncle had let him drive the family speeder a few times, but never alone, and only back and forth to Anchorhead. Luke had suggested to his uncle that it might be a good idea to buy a second speeder as a backup vehicle, but Owen said they didn't need more than one. Luke knew he'd have to come up with a much better reason for another speeder before he pestered his uncle again.

Meanwhile, and most fortunately, Biggs had his own landspeeder, and he enjoyed spur-of-the-moment jaunts just as much as Luke did. Biggs's speeder was an open-cockpit jalopy, an old Selanikio Sportster with a rebuilt Aratech Arrow engine that had a top speed of 250 kilometers per hour. Even resting motionless in the air, it purred loudly, as if it wanted to get moving.

Luke jumped into the front passenger seat. "Why're we still sitting here? Is this your landspeeder or your grandmother's?"

Biggs wiggled his fingers beside one ear, as if he were flicking an invisible irritation. "Did I just hear a joke?" he said. "Tell me, do you think my grandmother's speeder can do this?" He popped the clutch and stomped on the accelerator. The landspeeder tore off.

"Whoo-eee!" Luke shouted.

"Nice day for a ride!" Biggs shouted over the roar of his speeder's engine as he made a wide turn around Luke's home and headed north. "Where do you wanna go?"

"As far as we can get!"

Biggs grinned. "Would you settle for seeing the *Spice Siren*?"

Luke frowned. "Well, that's only about ninety klicks away."

Biggs laughed. "Would you rather I turned around?"

"Not a chance! I did extra chores yesterday so I could have today off. Let's get to the *Siren* already! Can't this heap go any faster?"

"Heap?! That tears it, Skywalker!" Biggs hit the brakes and brought the landspeeder to a sudden stop.

"Gosh, Biggs," Luke said as the speeder bobbed in the air over the desert's baked surface, the Lars homestead still visible behind them. "I was only joking."

"Joking?" Biggs shook his head. "Of all the nerve . . ." He jumped out of the speeder's cockpit and ran around the front of the vehicle to Luke's side. Staring hard at Luke, he said, "You just insulted my speeder for the last time."

Luke had never seen Biggs so angry. "Biggs, I'm sorry I said —"

"Don't waste your breath saying sorry to me," Biggs said. "If anyone deserves an apology, it's my speeder."

"Your . . . speeder?" Luke gasped. He couldn't believe how Biggs was overreacting. "Are you serious, or —"

"*Shh!*" Biggs interrupted. He leaned over the speeder's hood, placing his left ear close to its hot metal surface.

Concerned, Luke said, "Something wrong with the engine?"

Biggs raised his head from the hood, then shook his head. "She . . . she's crying, Luke. She said her heart's broken because some . . . some moisture farmer's nephew called her . . . a heap!" Biggs made a sad face that was too ridiculous to take seriously.

Luke burst into laughter. When he was done, he said, "You really had me going there, pal."

But Biggs wasn't finished. "She also said maybe you'd joke about her less . . . if I let you drive."

Luke started to laugh again, but then he saw the grin on Biggs's face. The laughter caught in Luke's throat. He gasped. "Really?"

Biggs gestured to the empty seat behind the speeder's controls. "Shove over, hotshot. My speeder's ready to go, and we ain't got all day."

Luke slid behind the controls and Biggs jumped into the passenger seat. As Luke gunned the engine, he decided for the millionth time that Biggs Darklighter really was the best friend anyone could ever have. He pressed the accelerator and they zoomed off.

The *Spice Siren* had once been a Republic freighter, but that was before it had crashed on Tatooine and been reduced to a large scrap heap. Although Jawa scavengers had picked the large wreck clean ages before, it had evolved into something of a minor tourist destination on Tatooine. Unfortunately, when Luke and Biggs arrived at the *Space Siren*'s final resting place, they found that it had attracted the wrong kind of tourists.

"Womp rats!" Luke said. The large omnivorous rodents were crawling all over the derelict.

"At least a dozen of 'em," Biggs said. "Careful, don't drive too close to the —"

Before Biggs could complete his warning, a womp rat leaped from the wreck's broken tail section and landed on the back of his speeder. Luke heard the loud thud behind him and stomped on the accelerator, launching the speeder forward and sending the womp rat skittering back against the speeder's central thruster. The womp rat dug its razor-sharp claws into the speeder's hull.

Biggs moved fast, twisting in his seat to grab his rifle just as the womp rat turned and opened its fanged jaws. Biggs fired an energy bolt directly into the womp rat's head, and it toppled off the back of the speeder.

Breathless, Luke said, "You all right?"

"Yeah," Biggs said. "Circle back. We can't let those womp rats become someone else's problem!"

It took them almost fifteen minutes to kill the remaining womp rats. They shot skillfully and efficiently, never leaving the safety of their vehicle until their last target had fallen. When they were done, they climbed out of the speeder to survey the carnage.

"Good thing we got here when we did," Luke said. "If some family had come to the *Siren* with kids . . . I hate to think what might have happened."

Biggs nodded. Toeing one of the carcasses, he said, "I've never seen womp rats this big outside of Beggar's Canyon."

Luke nodded. Beggar's Canyon was a long, winding channel of dried riverbeds that snaked through an area northeast of Mos Espa, and it was home to a notoriously large number of womp rats. Despite the verminous population, the canyon had long been a popular hangout for youths, a place to test their souped-up landspeeders and skyhoppers.

Luke said, "Think there might be more rats on the loose?"

"You can bet on it. We'd better report this to the officials in Anchorhead. But first, let's torch these carcasses before they attract more scavengers."

"The officials might not believe us. Maybe we should bring one rat back for proof?"

"Good idea."

They gathered the carcasses, dragging them away from the *Spice Siren*, and used some spare fuel to set all but one of the larger womp rats ablaze. After they loaded and strapped the remaining carcass onto the back of the speeder, Luke returned to the driver's seat and they took off.

As they traveled southeast along the edge of the Jundland Wastes, Biggs gestured to a break in the mountain range on the right and said, "Wanna take a little detour?"

"Into the Wastes?"

"Why not? We've got time."

Luke grinned and turned right.

The desert soon gave way to rockier terrain, but the speeder continued to travel as smoothly as it had over the even salt flats. Biggs patted the speeder's dashboard and said, "Handles great, doesn't she?"

"I'll say! So, when we get to Anchorhead, who should we tell —"

"Stop the speeder."

"Huh?"

"Just do it."

Biggs was looking off to the side. Luke wasn't sure whether his friend was joking around again, but he brought the speeder to a stop and cut the engine.

Biggs said, "Look thataway." He pointed toward the Wastes. "See? That row of little bumps between those two buttes?"

Luke followed Biggs's gaze and saw a long series of shadowy shapes. He watched them for a moment, then said, "They're moving."

"They're banthas," Biggs said. "At least twenty or so. Looks like they're moving in single file."

"It's so . . . orderly." Luke glanced at Biggs. "Think there's Sand People riding them?"

"Let's find out," Biggs said. He had a set of macrobinoculars clipped to his belt, and he removed them and held them up to his eyes.

Luke said, "Well?"

"See for yourself," Biggs said, handing the macrobinoculars to Luke.

Luke peered through the lenses and zoomed in on a bantha. On its back were two humanoid figures. He could see only their silhouettes, but then he saw a glint of metal on one figure's head. "Yep," he said. "Sand People."

"I wonder what they're up to." Keeping his eyes on the distant banthas, Biggs gestured at the speeder's controls and said, "Start her up again, then head for the left of that butte. Get us up to around one fifty until we're about two klicks from the butte, then kill the engine. We'll coast in quiet the rest of the way, get in close, and have a look without them seeing us first."

Luke looked at Biggs. "But what if they *do* see us first?"

Biggs flashed a toothy grin. "First, we smile pretty at them. Then we hope the engine starts up again and we leave very, very fast."

Luke followed Biggs's instructions and brought the coasting speeder to a silent stop near the base of the stratified butte. Beyond the butte, there was a wide, shallow valley. Luke and Biggs grabbed their laser rifles and left the speeder, staying low as they moved behind some rocks. They peered over the rocks, and they waited.

The banthas came into view a few minutes later, moving out from behind the next butte to proceed down into the valley. Luke shifted the macrobinoculars to the left of the procession and said, "They're heading for . . . I'm not sure what it is. A cluster of poles and arches? Maybe a fire pit?"

Biggs took the macrobinoculars. "Or ruins of some kind. Maybe a camp."

Luke watched the lead bantha wrap around their mysterious destination. The other banthas followed until they had formed a ring around the site, and then they came to a stop. Luke said, "What're they doing?"

"The visibility's not great," Biggs said, "but I think the Tuskens are dismounting. The banthas are just standing there. They're bunched so tight around whatever they're looking at I can't see what's going on."

"Let's just wait a little while," Luke said. "See what happens."

Several minutes later, the Tusken Raiders remounted the banthas and moved off in single file, continuing on their course away from Luke and Biggs. Luke said, "I wanna see what's down there."

"Me, too," Biggs said. "But let's stay put until they're farther away."

They waited until the banthas had traveled so far that they could barely be seen by the naked eye. They returned to Biggs's speeder. Biggs said, "I'll drive. You keep your rifle ready and your eyes peeled for any sign of a trap."

Biggs's speeder descended into the valley. As they drew closer to the place the Tusken Raiders had left, Luke realized that the arches and poles he'd seen earlier were made out of desiccated bantha bones. Bits of sun-bleached leather skins clung to some of the bones.

"Looks like an old Tusken camp, all right," Biggs said as he guided his speeder through a slow turn around the ruins.

Clutching his rifle, Luke rose in his seat to get a better look at the area. He kept his voice low as he said, "What do you think happened here?"

"You got me," Biggs said, "but whatever happened, it wasn't recent. Those bantha ribs are whiter than a . . . What in the name of —"

Luke's eyes locked on the same thing that had just caught Biggs's attention. In the sand surrounding the remains of one Tusken dwelling were a number of shattered humanoid skeletons.

Biggs slowed his speeder to a stop. "Look there," he said. "Those skulls . . . they're cut clean in half. The only thing I know of that can cut with that kind of precision is an industrial laser."

Luke hadn't noticed just how still the air was until a strangely cold breeze flowed over and past them, and he nearly jumped when he saw movement in the ruins. The breeze had blown a pair of leather strips that dangled from one of the arched ribs. Luke didn't wonder what the leather strips might have been used for. It didn't take much imagination to guess that the Tuskens had once used them to string someone up.

Luke felt his blood run cold, and an overwhelming sense of dread engulfed him. He tried to tear his gaze from the leather strips, and felt suddenly queasy when he realized he could not, as if he were compelled to keep staring at them. "Biggs," he whispered as he slid back down against his seat, "get us out of here."

"What's wrong?"

"Biggs," Luke said again, his voice almost a whimper as he forced himself to squeeze his eyes shut, "go . . . now . . . *please*."

"Sure, just take it easy." Biggs tapped the accelerator and they sped off, heading out of the Jundland Wastes.

Several minutes later, after they'd left the Wastes, Biggs stopped the speeder and looked at Luke. He said, "You okay?"

Luke nodded. "Sorry," he said. "I don't know what came over me. That place, it . . . it just made me feel so . . ."

"Scared?"

"Yeah," Luke said. Then he quickly added, "You're not gonna tell anyone, are ya?"

"Not if you don't tell anyone *I* was scared."

"Really? You, too?"

Biggs nodded. "I've seen some spooky stuff before, but *that* place. . . ? That was like a nightmare."

Luke nodded, but he thought, *No. It was worse.*

"Well, it's behind us now. And speaking of behind us . . ." Biggs glanced over his shoulder at the womp rat carcass strapped to the back of the speeder, then said, "Let's get this varmint to Anchorhead."

They drove off. Luke tried to focus on the land ahead of them but kept thinking of the ruins. He wondered if his uncle or aunt had ever heard about an abandoned Tusken camp in the Jundland Wastes, but he knew better than to ask. If his uncle learned that he had been out exploring the Wastes, he'd be grounded indefinitely.

After reporting their skirmish with the womp rats to the Anchorhead officials, Biggs returned Luke to the Lars homestead. It was almost evening when they arrived to find a rust-encrusted Jawa sandcrawler parked near the homestead's entry dome. Luke climbed out of Biggs's speeder. Then Biggs took off, heading back to his own family's farm.

Luke walked to the front of the sandcrawler and found his uncle engaged in conversation with a group of Jawas. Hearing Luke's approach, the Jawas turned their small, hooded heads to fix their glowing yellow eyes on the boy. The chief Jawa directed the others to get some equipment from inside the sandcrawler.

Luke stopped beside his uncle and said, "What's going on?"

"Just bought some more vaporators," Owen said. "I'm expanding the farm to the outlying ranges."

More vaporators? Luke's shoulders sagged as he thought of the additional work that would be required of him.

Owen said, "Something wrong?"

"No, sir." Luke turned and looked away from the sandcrawler. The dust that Biggs's speeder had kicked up while departing was still in the air.

Suddenly, an idea struck Luke.

He straightened his shoulders. Trying to sound casual, he said, "Uncle Owen, I think it's great that you're expanding the farm."

"Is that so?"

"Yeah, I always thought it was a shame, all that land of yours just sitting out there, not being used or generating income."

"Well, we're agreed on that."

"But I was wondering . . . how am I supposed to get to the outlying ranges? I mean, it's too far to walk. I'll need to get to the vaporators fast, even for routine maintenance." Lowering his voice so the Jawas wouldn't hear, he added, "And if we're going to stop scavengers from taking your property, I'll need to check the new vaporators more often too."

Owen's brow furrowed. "You're still trying to convince me we need another landspeeder."

Luke shrugged. "Well, unless you want to use the family speeder every time we need to check a —"

"I'll think about it," Owen said.

Yes! Luke believed that his uncle would soon realize that getting another speeder was not only practical, but necessary. He also knew from experience that it would be best not to push his luck any more on the subject, at least not for the day. Trying not to grin, he nodded, then turned and started walking to the entry dome.

The suns were close to the horizon. Looking beyond the homestead's courtyard, Luke saw long shadows crawling across the desert.

And then his gaze landed on the area of the unmarked graves that included his grandmother's final resting place.

He thought of the broken skeletons he'd seen at the abandoned Tusken camp. He suddenly found himself wondering which graveyard was more miserable. The one where the butchered remains of the dead had been left exposed for all to see? Or the one where the buried were already all but forgotten? Luke couldn't decide. Both were terribly unfortunate fates.

But as Luke descended to his underground home, he knew one thing for certain. As bad as life could be on Tatooine, death was usually worse.

CHAPTER FIVE

Luke was moving fast over the desert in his land-speeder, heading back home from Anchorhead, when he sighted yet another womp rat running toward some rocks. He had one hand on the speeder's controls and the other wrapped around the grip of his laser rifle, its barrel extended away from the vehicle. He didn't bother to reduce speed as he took aim and squeezed the weapon's trigger.

"Yee-oww!" Luke hollered with excitement when he saw the fired energy bolt strike the vile womp rat, killing it instantly. He was amazed by his own shot, and he doubted that Biggs had ever made a one-handed bull's-eye while driving a speeder.

It was Luke's seventeenth year on Tatooine. Although he still dreamed of adventure elsewhere, he was enjoying life more than ever. Two years earlier, his uncle had finally agreed to let him buy the used open-cockpit X-34 landspeeder that he now drove. Luke was also the proud owner of a used Incom T-16 skyhopper, a tri-wing, ion engine-equipped airspeeder that he used for trans-orbital jumps and racing through Beggar's Canyon. Biggs Darklighter had a skyhopper, too, as did most of their friends. Both Biggs and Luke had armed their T-16s with laser cannons in their ongoing effort to keep down the womp rat population.

Raiding storehouses and gnawing through moisture vaporator cables, womp rats had become an increasingly big problem on Tatooine — so big that the government of Anchorhead and the regional members of Affiliated Moisture Farmers had passed a bounty ordinance that paid out ten credits per rat. Luke and Biggs were pouring most of their earnings into upgrading their T-16s.

Luke parked the landspeeder so he could run and collect the womp rat he'd just killed. He tossed the carcass into the back of his speeder, then jumped into the vehicle and took off. As he drove home, it occurred to him that the bounty on the womp rat might pay for a set of macrobinoculars he'd been wanting.

Luke arrived at the Lars homestead, parked his landspeeder, and ran down to the courtyard. "Uncle Owen! Aunt Beru! I'm home!"

"Late!" Owen bellowed as he rose from the table in the dining alcove. "And without the rebuilt parts for our Treadwell, even though you took all day!"

Owen had sent Luke to get some refurbished parts for a Treadwell droid at Tosche Station in Anchorhead, where Luke's friend Fixer worked as a mechanic. Unfortunately, Fixer claimed that he had become overwhelmed by several other jobs. Luke had known that his uncle would not be pleased that he was returning from Anchorhead with only a dead womp rat to show for his time away from the farm.

Luke saw his aunt emerge from the kitchen, but returned his gaze to his uncle. "I tried giving Fixer a hand, Uncle Owen," he said feebly, "but with his backlog, he says it'll be a week before —"

"Without that droid," Owen said, "we can't install those new vaporators."

"I *know*, Uncle Owen," Luke said. "And I kinda wondered . . . Biggs Darklighter's leaving soon for the Academy, and tomorrow, the gang's planning a sort of farewell celebration. Until the droid's working, I can't *do* much, so —"

"So it'll be an excuse to idle away more time," Owen grumbled. "Luke, a moisture farmer can't —"

"Owen," Beru interrupted, "Biggs is Luke's best friend. He'll be gone a year or more. You let a brother leave without saying good-bye. Haven't you wished —"

"Enough, Beru!" Owen snapped. He scowled, then looked at Luke.

Luke held his breath, waiting for his uncle's decision.

Owen let out a defeated sigh. "You can go, young man," he said. "But don't ask for anything else until we have a functioning Treadwell. And if any vaporators break down . . ."

"Oh, they won't, sir," Luke said. "I promise."

Owen walked off across the courtyard, leaving Luke with Beru in the dining alcove. Luke shook his head as he followed his aunt into the kitchen. "Gee," he said, "I never figured Uncle Owen would give in. What *happened* between him and my father?"

Beru turned her back to Luke while she began slicing vegetables at the counter. "Er . . . nothing really, Luke," she said. "Perhaps . . . Owen just . . . depended too much on your father staying with him on the farm."

"Like he does now with me?" Luke leaned against the counter and looked at the floor. "Whenever I mention going to the Academy like Biggs, he —"

"He *cares* for you, Luke," Beru said, then added, "in his own gruff way."

"I guess I know that," Luke said. "And all his effort on the farm is to build something for us all. Makes me feel like a traitor to even think about leaving, Aunt Beru. Still . . . some crazy part of me keeps feeling like there should be more." He shook his head. "Maybe I'm just afraid to grow up, to face responsibility like Uncle Owen. What *else* could it be?"

He looked at his aunt and found her returning his gaze with a sad smile. Neither one of them knew what to say.

Luke drifted toward the tech dome so he could do a maintenance check on his skyhopper. He wanted to make sure it was thoroughly tuned before the next day, when he aimed to fly his best against Biggs at Beggar's Canyon.

"Hey, Biggs!" Luke said into his skyhopper's comm. "Over here!" Luke had just zoomed in from the south when he spotted Biggs's magenta T-16 whipping through the sky over Beggar's Canyon.

"I see you waggling your wings, hotshot," Biggs answered. "Glad you could make it. But just 'cause this is the last get-together of the two Shooting Stars, don't expect any breaks when the run begins!"

Luke grinned. *We're two Shooting Stars that can't be stopped.* Biggs had come up with that line, as well as the name for their very exclusive club, after the local authorities announced that each of them had shot more womp rats than any other bounty collector. Because Biggs happened to know that it annoyed Luke when anyone over the age of seven didn't know the proper name for meteors, Biggs couldn't resist joking, "We may never be meteors, but we'll always be Shooting Stars."

Biggs maneuvered his skyhopper so he was flying parallel with Luke, so close that Luke could clearly see

Biggs's mustached face. As they circled over the mouth of the canyon, several more skyhoppers came into view. Luke instantly recognized the vehicles piloted by Windy Starkiller, Tosche Station's Fixer, and also Deak, another kid from Anchorhead.

One skyhopper was notably absent. Luke's friend Tank had recently left Tatooine to attend the Imperial Military Academy of Carida. Luke didn't know all the details, but he'd heard that Tank had failed to get into the Naval Academy on Prefsbelt IV, so it seemed doubtful that he'd wind up piloting starships for the Empire. This had surprised Luke, because he thought Tank was a pretty good pilot, at least in a skyhopper.

As Fixer's T-16 swept past him, Luke noticed that his airfoils had been freshly trimmed. *As if that'll make any difference,* Luke thought.

Ever since Biggs had set the speed record for Beggar's Canyon and simultaneously become the first pilot to successfully fly a skyhopper through the open hole at the top of the rock formation known as the Stone Needle, Fixer had become obsessed with modifying his own T-16 to beat Biggs's time. Luke wondered whether Fixer had been spending more hours working on his T-16 than refurbishing parts for a certain Treadwell droid.

Because the farewell party was for Biggs, the other pilots insisted that he choose their course. Biggs picked one of the more treacherous stretches, a twisting route through a ravine that terminated at a high wall, which loomed over the area's largest womp rat burrow. Luke knew that the course would test almost any pilot's nerve, but he wasn't surprised that none of the others backed out immediately. No one wanted to be called a coward.

The starting signal was given. All the skyhoppers power-dived into the yawning canyon mouth.

Through his triangular windshield, Luke saw his T-16's shadow ripple over the canyon's rocky floor as he hurtled forward. Biggs's magenta T-16 was just ahead of him. He increased speed as he dropped altitude, zooming so low that he could no longer see the shadow that traveled beneath him, then blasted past Biggs to grab the lead.

As the skyhoppers whipped around the first turn, Luke accidentally swung wide, leaving an opening for Biggs, who accelerated ahead of him. A warning light flashed beside a sensor scope on Luke's control console, indicating that his starboard airfoil was less than a meter from the canyon wall. Luke laughed as he swerved away from the wall and went after Biggs.

A wide boulder lay across the canyon floor. Biggs brought his T-16 up fast to avoid a collision, but as he ascended over the boulder, Luke accelerated again, sheering through the gap between the top of the boulder and the bottom of his friend's skyhopper. Luke let out a loud whoop as he reclaimed the lead.

There came another sharp turn, and then the distance between the walls narrowed before the next twist. Luke glanced at his scopes to see whether Biggs was gaining on him, and found that three skyhoppers had already pulled up and out of the race by ascending vertically from the canyon. Less than one kilometer of snaking turns later, he was still ahead of Biggs, and the last of the other pilots had pulled out.

The distance between the walls opened slightly. Biggs said, "Gangway, hotshot, I'm making my move!" He sped past Luke and swung in front of him.

"Just like I figured, Biggs, ol' buddy . . . just a hair too early!" Luke chuckled. "There's still time for me to jump you before the last turn, and no room for you to overtake me after that!"

But as they approached the last turn, Biggs suddenly braked with his retros, leaving Luke with no choice but to pull up or collide. As Luke sent his T-16 straight up and out of the canyon, he shouted, "Biggs, you tricky son of a gun!"

Luke swung back at an angle so he could look down and see Biggs make the final turn. Biggs's T-16's cannons fired, launching ground-charge missiles at the womp rat burrows, and then he elevated rapidly to escape the ravine's dead-end wall.

"Way to go, Biggs!" Luke said into his comm as his friend rocketed out of the canyon. "I wouldn't have dared to try what you did! Guess that's why you're headed for the Academy, and I'll probably stay on the moisture farm."

"Don't kid yourself," Biggs laughed. "You'll be at the Academy soon enough."

The other pilots had landed their skyhoppers on a plateau along the canyon's upper rim. Luke and Biggs parked beside them, and Luke was still congratulating Biggs on his finish as they walked over to Fixer, Windy, and Deak, who were gathered beside Fixer's skyhopper.

Luke noticed they were with Camie, a pretty girl with dark hair, who had been hanging out at Tosche Station more and more lately. Camie was standing near Deak, her hand on his back. Luke had been nursing a crush on Camie for some time. Seeing her beside Deak, Luke couldn't help feeling jealous.

"Look sharp, Camie," Deak said as Luke and Biggs approached. "Here they come. 'Two Shooting Stars that can't be stopped.'" He said this in a whiny voice, making fun of the pair.

"That's what we always say, Deak," Biggs said affably. "And I didn't see anyone else proving us wrong today."

"Now that you mention it, Biggs," Luke said, "I don't recall seeing Deak anywhere near the finish."

Fixer said, "That's because Deak was the first one to leave the race."

Camie looked at Deak and said, "Is that true?"

Deak said, "Well, I, uh, wanted to come back and see you, doll."

"Oh, yeah?" Camie said. She stepped away from Deak. She didn't even glance at Luke as she breezed past him and sidled up to Fixer. Looking back at Deak, Camie said, "From now on, *doll*, you can see me from a distance."

Fixer grinned.

Luke thought, *Does Camie like Fixer?*

Windy said, "So, Biggs, after you graduate from the Academy, are you gonna go straight into the Imperial Navy?"

Biggs shrugged. "I'm not crazy about taking orders from anyone, but if joining the Navy is the surest way to become a licensed starpilot, then I'll just suffer through it."

Fixer said, "There might be another option, Biggs. From what I've heard, you don't need a license to join the Rebellion. They'll take anyone. Ha!"

Deak, Windy, and Camie laughed at this too. Luke just smiled sheepishly. In recent months, he had heard various rumors about the fledgling Rebel Alliance, which reportedly opposed the Galactic Empire and accused the Emperor of numerous atrocities. He looked at Biggs, wondering how his friend would respond to Fixer's remark.

"Can't say I know much about the Rebellion," Biggs said, "but I think anyone who challenges the Empire is either very brave or very stupid."

"Oh, *definitely* very stupid," Windy said. "Anyone who takes a potshot at the Emperor is just looking to die."

"Could be," Biggs said. "Anyway, it's not like anyone on Tatooine has reason to worry. The Empire's a long, long way from here, and so is any rebellion against it. But why are we talking about this? Is this a farewell celebration, or is this a —"

Before Biggs could finish, the group heard the roar of a repulsorlift engine. They all turned fast to see a landspeeder approaching over the plateau. Spewing smoke and flames, the speeder careened toward the landed skyhoppers, then swerved and smashed into an outcropping of gray rock.

With several other youths at their heels, Luke and Biggs ran to the crashed speeder. Luke was first to arrive at the side of the speeder's driver, who'd been thrown from the vehicle and lay sprawled on the hard ground. Noticing the driver's uniform, Luke said, "Biggs, he's a Militia Scout!"

Although Tatooine was a largely lawless world, regional militia units patrolled the outskirts of the more civilized areas to watch for Tusken Raiders and other threats. Biggs knelt beside the man and said, "Easy, mister. You're okay now."

"No!" the man said. "Got to warn everyone . . . big trouble!"

The man's eyelids fluttered, and then his hand lashed out to grip Biggs's arm. Luke could tell that the man was in shock and trying not to pass out.

"Tusken Raiders on the rampage!" the wounded man continued. "Lot of 'em . . . mad as rock hornets! A supply caravan accidentally polluted one of their sacred wells!"

Biggs grimaced. "What kind of fools would do that?"

"Fools smuggling blasters . . ." the man continued. "Sand People got the smugglers *and* the guns! They're well-armed and angry enough to hit Anchorhead and any farms in between! They weren't far behind me, so —"

The man was interrupted by the sound of long-range blasterfire. A millisecond later, one of the landed sky-hoppers erupted into a fireball. Luke was stunned as he looked at the burning skyhopper. He was relieved that the skyhopper had been empty, and also that it wasn't his.

"Everyone to cover!" Biggs shouted as more shots were fired. "They're here!"

As one group of youths dragged the wounded man beside the outcropping, another ran to their vehicles to grab their own blaster rifles. Fixer tossed rifles to Luke and Biggs, who threw themselves down behind some rocks to return fire, sending energized bolts back across the desert. Luke couldn't see the enemy, but as more blasterfire hammered against the rocks that protected him and his friends, he had no doubt that they were up against at least a dozen Sand People.

Luke glanced to his right and saw Windy hunkered over a portable comm unit that he'd hauled to the rocks. Luke said, "Windy, any luck with the communicator?"

"Too much atmospheric interference," Windy said. "Gotta wait till the suns are lower."

Hearing this, Biggs faced Luke and said, "By that time, the main party could be in Anchorhead! The gang's handling this fine, Luke. You game to try for one of the hoppers?"

"When my uncle's place is one of those in danger?" Luke said. "Try an' stop me!"

Taking the rifles with them, Luke and Biggs ran as fast as they could for Luke's skyhopper. As they ran, blaster shots slammed into the ground near their feet. They were more than halfway to the skyhopper, moving past another rocky outcropping, when Luke saw a masked humanoid form rise suddenly away from the rocks.

"Biggs!" Luke shouted.

And then Biggs saw it too. A Tusken Raider, standing on the rocks less than three meters away from them, close enough that they could smell his filthy robes. He was clutching a gaderffi, a long metal weapon with a sharp-tipped spear on one end and a blunt club on the other. He was poised to attack.

Although Luke and Biggs were carrying rifles, they both knew that Tuskens were notoriously fast. There was a definite possibility that the Tusken might deal a deadly blow with his gaderffi before either of them could fire a shot.

Biggs muttered, "Blast them and their ability to pop up out of nowhere." He placed one foot forward, bracing himself to jump back, as he said, "Move away from me, Luke, so instead of swinging that gaderffi, he'll be forced to throw —"

Biggs was still talking as the Tusken flung the gaderffi. Biggs tried to dodge it. He failed.

"No!" Luke shouted as the gaderffi struck Biggs. Biggs stumbled back, and the heavy spear fell away from his body.

Luke's reflexes took over, bringing his rifle up fast at the same time that the Tusken lunged at him. Luke squeezed the trigger. The blast caught the Tusken in the chest, and the masked figure collapsed in a heap against the rocks.

"Good shootin', hotshot," Biggs said as Luke helped him to his feet. "He only got my shoulder." Suddenly, Biggs trembled. "But from the way I f-feel, that point may have been dipped in sand bat venom."

"Hang on, Biggs," Luke said, helping him walk to the skyhopper.

As Luke eased Biggs into the cockpit and squeezed onto the seat beside him, he looked at the wound on his friend's shoulder. "I'll have you to a medi-droid before that stuff can do any damage," he said. He fired the T-16's engine. "I'm boosting us straight up and out of here!"

"No, Luke," Biggs said through clenched teeth as the T-16 lifted off. "Stay low. They're better armed than usual, remember? Try for altitude and we're a sitting duck for their long-range blasters!"

Just then a blaster bolt tore through the air in front of the T-16. Luke realized that Biggs was right. He pushed at the controls, doing his best to take evasive action.

Biggs said, "You're going to have to stay down . . . go through the mountains . . . 'stead'a over them."

"Through?" Luke said. "Biggs, there's no way except . . ."

"Yeah," Biggs said. "Diablo Cut! No one's ever done it before. Probably for the good reason that it's impossible! But if we take time to go the long way round, some farms and part of Anchorhead may not be waiting!"

Although Biggs hadn't mentioned it, Luke could think of another reason to avoid a longer route. The way Biggs was sweating, Luke had no doubt that the gaderf-fi's tip had indeed been poisoned, and that the poison was already working through Biggs's system. Unless they took a shortcut, Biggs might not survive.

Luke sent the T-16 into a steep plunge, into a narrow ravine. "Okay, Mr. Darklighter," Luke said. "Diablo Cut it is! Somebody's gotta be first. Why not us?"

The T-16 hurtled through the twisting ravine. Luke banked hard to wrap around one curve, only to find himself confronting another sharp turn, and then another after that. Hoping to avoid being sighted by any trigger-happy Sand People, he tried to stay below the shafts of sunlight that clung to the upper edges of the ravine's high walls.

Luke descended closer to the shadowy canyon floor. As he banked around a rock formation, his weight shifted to his right, accidentally pressing against Biggs's injured arm. Biggs groaned. Luke kept his eyes forward and sent the T-16 around the next turn.

"Luke . . ." Biggs gasped. "I must've been crazy . . . to get you into this. It can't be . . . done. . . . It . . ."

Biggs fainted.

Luke saw what looked like a dark spot at the base of a cliff. He and Biggs had visited the area before, and he recognized the "spot" as the reason no skyhopper pilot had ever dared fly through Diablo Cut before. It was the entrance to a cavern system that cut under and through Beggar's Canyon. The ground outside the cavern was littered with the remnants of old Podracers.

Luke angled the T-16 into a steep dive, pulled up fast, and then leveled off to fly straight into the cave. He was immediately engulfed in total darkness.

Warning lights flashed on the T-16's console. Luke tore his gaze from his triangular windshield and locked his eyes on the sensor scopes. The scopes detected a deadly curtain of stalactites in his path. Luke sent the skyhopper between two stalactites, then veered around a third.

The warning lights continued to flash. Luke kept his gaze fixed on the scopes as he quickly adjusted the thrusters and lifted his port airfoil to avoid a collision with another underground rock formation. A moment later, he was weaving desperately between natural columns of stone.

The scopes displayed what resembled a smooth-walled straightaway. Luke guessed it was an ancient lava tube and accelerated into it, racing even faster through the darkness. Luke thought, *This really is crazy.*

The tube emptied into a wide chamber, and then Luke's scopes picked up what looked like an exit, an opening in the ceiling at the chamber's far end. Luke risked a glance through the windshield to see a jagged crack of pale blue light. Even though Biggs was unconscious, Luke said, "Open sky above us, Biggs! We're through!"

But as he steered the T-16 up through the opening, he received an unexpected greeting. A Tusken Raider scouting party was waiting outside the cavern, and, hearing his skyhopper's approach, they raised their pilfered blaster rifles and fired.

Luke angled up and away from the Tuskens, but a moment later he heard a hammering sound from behind as blasterfire struck one of the T-16's afterburners. He knew that the skyhopper was bound to catch fire from the assault, but he held tight to the controls as he launched forward at top speed, heading southwest.

He rocketed over the Mospic High Range and Bestine and was angling toward Anchorhead when a warning light flashed. His starboard airfoil was on fire. As smoke trailed from behind the T-16, he feared the craft might explode. He knew that his best chance to prevent an explosion was to plow the skyhopper into the sand, and not near a heavily populated area.

He suddenly realized he was no longer angling for Anchorhead. As if by instinct, he was heading home.

He saw the Lars homestead ahead and dropped the skyhopper at the perimeter. He winced as the starboard airfoil sheared off, and then the T-16 skidded across the sand before it came to a shuddering stop.

Luke threw the hatch open and pulled Biggs out. He was carrying Biggs to the homestead's entry dome when he saw his uncle running toward him.

"Luke!" Owen shouted. "Have you gone mad, young man?"

"Get a medpac for Biggs, Uncle Owen," Luke said. "An' have Aunt Beru call out the local militia *fast!*"

There were various causes for celebration on Tatooine that day, at least for the human population, excluding the smugglers who were killed by Tusken Raiders. Although there had still been some atmospheric interference, Aunt Beru was able to get a comm message to Anchorhead. The local militia — with the help of some rambunctious kids and their skyhoppers — drove off the Tuskens from Beggar's Canyon and the surrounding areas and also recovered most of the stolen blasters. Although a landspeeder and a skyhopper had been destroyed at Beggar's Canyon, the wounded militia officer and the reckless young pilots all lived to fight and fly again.

Thanks to his friend Luke Skywalker and a fast-acting antitoxin, Biggs Darklighter made a swift and full recovery. As for Luke's skyhopper, that would require more effort to be restored.

But then Biggs left for the Academy. And Luke felt more stuck on the sand planet than ever before.

CHAPTER SIX

Windy poked around the cramped cockpit of Luke's refurbished T-16 skyhopper and said, "Where're your macrobinoculars?"

"I forget," Luke lied as he guided the skyhopper toward Beggar's Canyon. He knew exactly where he'd hidden the macrobinoculars so Windy wouldn't get his grubby hands on them.

Luke glanced at a sensor scope and saw that two other skyhoppers had already arrived at his destination. *Only two*, he thought. He knew that the vehicles belonged to Fixer and Deak.

A year had passed since Biggs and Tank had left Tatooine. Luke missed Biggs especially and still wasn't used to the absence of his best friend's skyhopper at the infrequent get-togethers with other young people. He wondered where Biggs was now.

Normally, Windy would have flown his own sky-hopper to Beggar's Canyon. According to Windy, his skyhopper had been "acting up," which was why he had accompanied his parents on their visit to the Lars homestead — so he could hitch a ride with Luke to meet up with the rest of the gang.

Windy saw the two skyhoppers on Luke's sensor scope. He said, "Looks like Fixer and Deak beat us."

Luke laughed. "It's not like we were racing to *get* here, Windy."

Ignoring Luke's comment, Windy said, "It's an easy bet we'll see Camie too. She and Fixer are practically glued to each other."

"Huh," Luke said, as if he couldn't care less. He did his best not to think about Camie, who'd encouraged the others to call him Wormie, and for no good reason that he could think of.

Luke landed his skyhopper near the other two. As he and Windy climbed out, Windy said, "Thanks for the lift. I owe you."

"Don't mention it," Luke said as he closed the skyhopper's hatch.

They found Fixer, Camie, and Deak a short distance from the parked skyhoppers, in the shade of a rocky wall, where they had set up some folding chairs and a portable cooler. Fixer was just popping the lid on a beverage container when Windy and Luke arrived. "Hey, everybody," Luke said. "Where's the party?"

"Wherever *I* am, Luke," Fixer said. Turning to his girlfriend, he added, "Right, Camie?"

Camie pursed her lips and blew a kiss at Fixer. Luke thought, *Oh, brother.*

Windy said, "Hey, boys, guess what Skywalker was doing?"

"Hey!" Luke said. "*Shh!*" He wished Windy would keep his mouth shut, but like most of his wishes, this one didn't come true.

"Sitting in the tech dome," Windy continued, "playing an Academy recruitment tape!"

Everyone jeered. "I was not," Luke lied. In fact, he had been listening to the tape that came with the Applicant's Information Packet from the Imperial Space Academy when Windy had arrived at the Lars homestead. When he had heard Windy entering the tech dome, he hadn't been able to switch off the tape and hide it fast enough. It wasn't that Luke was ashamed of wanting to go to the Academy, but that he resented how everyone teased him about his desire to become a starpilot. He gave Windy a dirty look and thought, *You can find your own way home.*

"You never change, Skywalker," Fixer said. "That all you want out of life, to parade around in a fancy uniform?"

Luke snapped, "So what do you want that's so much better, Fixer?"

"Hey, you watch it, boy!" Fixer said. "Just because you got lucky on a couple of crummy tests, that doesn't make you some kind of junior space explorer."

Shaking his head, Luke said, "I never said I was any better than y —"

Fixer interrupted, "You know what *I* did back when they made me take those exams? I walked in, filled out my name, and walked out again. *I* showed 'em."

Everyone but Luke seemed to find Fixer's claim impressive as well as amusing. Windy waved dismissively at Luke and said, "Just because he can answer fancy trick questions and do schoolbook flight maneuvers, he thinks it makes him better than us."

"I do not," Luke protested.

Facing Luke, Fixer said, "So you happened to qualify? So what? What do ya think you are, Biggs or something?"

"Yeah," Camie said, laughing. "He just wants to go to the Academy because Biggs did. He always was his hero." The way she said *hero* made it sound like something foul.

Luke felt his face flush as he tried to ignore Camie. He kept his gaze on Fixer and said, "Yeah, I'd like to go to the Academy. Why shouldn't I?"

"Because it's for suckers, Skywalker!" Fixer said. "They want to stick you into a uniform and give you orders. At least at the power station, I'm my own boss."

Windy said, "Anyway, my father says the Empire's just recruiting more people into the academies so they can draft them into the starfleet."

Deak looked down his nose at Luke and said, "Do you think *anybody* out there cares about *Luke Skywalker?*"

"If you leave home," Camie added, "nobody knows you."

Fixer drained his beverage container. "Hey, where is the juice?"

As Camie handed Fixer another drink, Luke said, "So, what's on the program for today, Fixer?"

"Speed runs, Skywalker," Fixer said. "Speed runs."

"Oh?"

"Gonna see how much time I can shave off the back stretch."

Windy said, "There's no way you can cut much more time off your lap, Fix. You're almost matching Biggs's best time around Beggar's Canyon as it is."

"Yeah, well, Biggs isn't here, and I am!" Fixer bellowed. "I'm as good as he ever was!"

"Oh, yeah?" Luke said. "Well, then why don't you thread the Stone Needle like Biggs did? That ought to take five seconds or better off your time."

Camie gasped. Although Luke had sounded pleasant,

as if he were casually offering advice to a friend, Camie knew that he had just proposed a very dangerous challenge to Fixer. Deak and Windy knew it too and looked at Fixer to see his reaction.

Fixer squinted at Luke and said, "Yeah? And Biggs is the only one who ever flew through it at racing speed, is that what you're saying?"

Luke chuckled. "No, I was just saying that if you want to improve your time, you —"

"You're crazy, Luke!" Camie said, glaring at him. "Why don't you guys go buzz the womp rats and take a few potshots at them? This speed run stuff is gonna get somebody killed."

"Hey, hey, hey," Fixer said. "What's the matter, Camie? You don't think I can do it? Listen, anything the great Biggs Darklighter could do, *I* can do."

"I never said you couldn't," Camie said, trying to placate her boyfriend.

"Yeah," Windy said, "nobody was knocking you, Fixer."

"Besides," Fixer said, "I don't need any shortcuts."

I knew he'd make some excuse, Luke thought. He smirked as he looked away from Fixer. Unfortunately, Fixer noticed.

"Hey!" Fixer said. "Do you wanna try and keep up with me?"

"Oh, Fixer," Camie said, shaking her head with disgust.

Still gazing at Luke, Fixer said, "Huh?"

Luke looked back at Fixer. "What?" Luke said. "*Me?*"

Fixer leered at him. "What, are you scared, Wormie?"

Luke exhaled. He knew that Fixer was just an overgrown jerk and that it was stupid to let the guy get under his skin. But with everyone looking at him, expecting him to back down, Luke wasn't in the mood to think reasonably. He said, "Yeah. All right. You're on!"

"Hoo, boy!" Deak laughed. "Wormie against the Fixer! That's gonna be a slaughter!"

Luke scowled. "Well, then *you* can ride with Fixer, Deak!" He turned for the door. "What're we waiting for, boys? Let's go!"

"Fixer!" Camie shouted as the four young men walked off. "Come back here, Fixer!" she hollered from beside the folding chairs. "I want this to stop right now!"

No one paid any attention to her.

Windy was scrunched inside the cockpit of Luke's T-16, poking around as he tried to find the macrobinoculars Luke had concealed. As Luke squeezed in behind the skyhopper's controls, Fixer's voice crackled over his comm. "Good luck, Skywalker," Fixer said. "See you in the tight spots!"

"Hey," Windy said, "I couldn't find those macrobinoculars anywhere."

"Never mind, Windy," Luke said. "Buckle up."

Luke revved the T-16's engines. He had adjusted the thrust sequence for extra boost, and the noise was phenomenal. Hearing the racket, Windy said, "Hey, what're you doing!"

"I'm standing in for Biggs!" Luke said. "Brace yourself."

Luke's skyhopper shuddered as it lifted slowly off the ground. Over the comm, Fixer said, "Here we go. One run down the back stretch, Skywalker, whenever you're ready."

Windy was reaching for the T-16's sissy bar only to discover that Luke had removed it. "Hey, wait a minute!" he said. "You and Fixer in the bottleneck together? Count me out!"

Luke gestured to the hatch and said, "Well, jump!" But because they were already hovering several meters above the ground, he wasn't surprised that Windy remained seated.

Fixer said, "Fall in even with me, Skywalker, and we'll let 'er rip."

Luke maneuvered his skyhopper so it hovered in the air beside Fixer's. As soon as Luke was in position, Fixer said, "Okay, hit it!"

Twin clouds of dust exploded from behind the two skyhoppers as they tore off into the canyon. As Luke accelerated and swung unnervingly close to the canyon's wall, Windy groaned loudly, then shrieked, "Look out!"

"Will you shut up and keep still!" Luke snapped.

Suddenly, Fixer's skyhopper zoomed forward and slid in front of Luke.

"Aw, no!" Luke said as he tapped his brakes to avoid flying straight into Fixer's thrusters. "You distracted me, Windy! Now Fixer's got the lead!"

"Well, let him keep it!" Windy shouted. "I want to live!"

From the comm, Fixer laughed and said, "How does my afterblast feel, Luke?"

The canyon corridor seemed to be rapidly closing in around them. Luke held tight to the controls as he searched for any way around Fixer's skyhopper, his eyes darting from his scopes to the high-speed blur in front of his canopy. Angry with himself for having fallen behind, Luke said, "It's too narrow to get past him!"

Windy said, "Whatever you do, don't go for altitude! Don't go for altitude! The crosswinds will smash us right into the canyon wall!"

Fixer's voice crackled. "Just make yourself comfortable back there, farm boy! It'll all be over in a minute!"

Luke snarled, "That's what *you* think!" He brought his T-16 up fast and veered around a rocky outcropping.

"Wha — Wait!" Windy gasped from behind. "Hey, you idiot! You took the wrong turn! You're headed for the Stone Needle!"

"Yeah," Luke said. "I bet we shave five seconds off our time."

"You're gonna kill us both!"

The Stone Needle came into view. As the distance closed between the skyhopper's nose and the Needle's jagged opening, Luke instinctively realized he was going too fast. With his left hand, he reached for a switch to cut power and shut down the afterburners, and the T-16 decelerated and dropped slightly. Then Luke kicked on the power again.

"There's no going back now," Luke said as the T-16 closed with the opening. "Stay gripped, Windy!"

The skyhopper was suddenly buffeted by crosswinds. Windy yelled, *"No-oooo!"*

Luke clutched the controls with almost crushing strength as he kept his trajectory for the opening. As the skyhopper tore through the Needle, Luke let out a whoop of excitement that was so loud he almost drowned out a series of nasty thuds, the sound of metal grinding and breaking against stone.

Incredibly, they were still airborne.

"We made it!" Luke said. "Windy, open your eyes! We made it!"

"I-I'm alive," Windy stammered. "I don't believe

it." Then he braved a glance at Luke's console. "Hey! Your stabilizer's gone!"

Luke felt the skyhopper begin to lean hard to the port side. Tugging at the controls to compensate for the lean, he said, "I can hold her. We've still got to cross that finish line."

"You'll crash us!"

"Here we go. . . ."

Luke saw the end of the course and revved down the engine for landing. The skyhopper hit the ground at a slight angle, jolting Luke and Windy, then bounced over the finish line before it hit the ground again. Luke's skyhopper kicked up a wide spray of dust as it slid to a stop.

"I *told* you I could bring her in," Luke said as the engines died down. Catching his breath, he added, "Hey . . . Windy . . . we won!" He laughed. "We *won!*"

"Won?" Windy gasped. "Luke, you're crazy. Crazy! I'm riding home with one of the others." He scrambled out of his seat and opened the hatch. "You're just an accident looking for a place to happen."

Luke was still laughing wildly as Windy staggered away from the skyhopper. He tilted his head back and said, "Oh, Biggs, you should've been here!"

CHAPTER SEVEN

Luke was on the south range of his uncle's moisture farm, working alongside a WED Treadwell droid to repair a broken moisture vaporator, when his eye caught a bright sparkle in the morning sky. Stepping away from the vaporator, he removed his macrobinoculars from his utility belt to get a better look.

He spotted two points of light and quickly adjusted his macrobinoculars' magnification. Although the two points remained indistinct, he could tell that they were starships, and that one was considerably larger than the other. Pulses of light flashed near and around the smaller ship.

Luke realized he was witnessing a space battle. He could hardly believe his eyes. Lowering his macrobinoculars, he glanced at the Treadwell droid and said, "Come on, Treadwell. Get yourself over to the landspeeder. I've gotta get into Anchorhead and tell Fixer about this!"

The Treadwell droid was right in the middle of making an adjustment to the vaporator. It swiveled its binocular photoreceptors to watch Luke run to the landspeeder that was parked a short distance away, and emitted a flurry of protesting beeps.

Although Luke didn't know exactly what the droid had just said, he recognized the tone well enough to understand that it was reluctant to stop working. He said, "Well, get it in gear, will ya?"

Like most of the equipment owned by Owen Lars, the droid was in need of repair, so Luke wasn't totally surprised when its engine suddenly exploded in a spray of sparks. As white smoke poured out of the Treadwell's engine, the spindly-necked droid beeped furiously.

"Stay put, then," Luke said. "I'll pick you up on the way home." He hopped into his landspeeder and took off across the desert, heading west for Anchorhead.

"I've told you kids to slow down!" an old woman hollered as she shook her fist after the landspeeder, which raced at a ridiculously fast speed toward Tosche Station. Luke swerved and brought his vehicle to a sudden stop, kicking up a wave of sand and dust.

He leaped out of the speeder and ran into the pourstone building, taking his macrobinoculars with him. Entering the station's sales office, he found Fixer seated with Camie, behind a cluttered table. Fixer was asleep, and Camie looked like she was just waking up. Luke picked up a piece of scrap from the table and tossed it at Fixer, but Camie's hand darted out to swat the scrap to the floor. The sudden movement made Fixer's eyes pop open.

"C'mon, shape it up, you guys!" Luke said as he moved toward the adjoining room, where Windy and Deak stood facing each other over a large console as they played a computer game. Beside Deak, another man stood with his back to Luke. The man had dark hair and wore a cape over a drab uniform, and he looked like . . . "Biggs?"

Biggs Darklighter turned with a broad grin on his face. He threw his arms around Luke, who exclaimed, "Hey! I didn't know you were back! When did you get in?"

"Just now!" Biggs said, beaming as he stepped back to look at Luke. "I never expected you to be out *working*!"

They both laughed at this. Luke didn't notice any obvious change in Biggs's appearance, so he said, "The Academy didn't change you much. . . . Oh, I almost forgot. There's a battle going on! Right here in our system! Come and look!"

Hearing Luke mention a battle, Deak groaned, "Not again! Forget it!"

Windy said, "Hey, what's all the noise about?"

As Briggs left the computer console, Deak pointed to him and said, "Did you come back down here to play the game?"

Luke ignored Deak and Windy and headed for the exit with Biggs right behind him. As Fixer and Camie followed them out, Camie muttered, "I think Wormie's caught too much sun."

Luke led the others onto the elevated terrace that wrapped around the station. While Fixer and Camie raised their hands to shield their eyes from the sun, Luke trained his macrobinoculars high into the sky and resighted the pinpoints of light. "There they are!" he said, then quickly handed the macrobinoculars to Biggs.

"Let's see," Biggs said. He craned his neck back and gazed up through the powerful lenses. A moment later, he said, "That's no battle, hotshot . . . they're just sitting there!" Handing the macrobinoculars back to Luke, he added, "Probably a freighter-tanker refueling."

"But there was a lot of firing earlier," Luke said. He was about to look through his macrobinoculars again when Camie snatched them from his hand. Annoyed, Luke said, "Hey!"

While Camie looked through the macrobinoculars, Biggs said, "I tell you, Luke, the Rebellion is a long way from here. *This* planet . . . ?" He shrugged. "Big hunk of nothing."

Fixer added, "I doubt the Empire would even fight to save this system."

Biggs headed back into the station with Fixer right behind him. Camie lowered the macrobinoculars and casually tossed the expensive device to Luke. Luke reached fast to catch them, but they nearly slipped from his fingers. Glaring at Camie, he snapped, "You watch it!"

As Camie walked back inside, Luke cast another glance upward and thought, *I know it was a battle. I'm sure of it!*

Later, after getting some drinks at Tosche Station's small cantina, Luke and Biggs walked outside. Luke was just finishing his account of his most recent race at Beggar's Canyon.

"So I cut my power," Luke said, "shut down the afterburners. . . . I was so close, I thought I was going to fry my instruments. As it was, I busted up the skyhopper pretty bad. Uncle Owen? Furious! He wound up grounding me for the rest of the season." He chucked Biggs on the shoulder. "You should have been there! It was fantastic!"

"You ought to take it a little easy, Luke," Biggs said. "You may be the hottest bush pilot this side of Mos Eisley, but those little skyhoppers are dangerous. Keep it up, one day . . . whammo! You're gonna end up a dark spot on the down side of a canyon wall."

"Look who's talking," Luke said, grinning. "You've been hanging around the starfleet so long you're beginning to sound like my uncle. You know, you're getting a little soft in the city. . . ."

Biggs gave Luke a playful shove. "I've missed you, kid."

"Yeah, well, things haven't been the same without you, Biggs." Luke kicked at the ground. "It's been so quiet."

Biggs glanced over his shoulder to make sure no one else was in earshot, then said, "Luke, I didn't come back just for a visit." He looked at the ground for a moment, then lifted his gaze to Luke. "I shouldn't tell you this, but you're the only one I can trust. See, I may never come back, and I just want someone to know."

Luke just stood there, looking at Biggs, wondering what had brought on his friend's sudden seriousness. Confused and alarmed, he said, "What are you talking about?"

Biggs threw another cautious glance over his shoulder, then looked back at Luke. Lowering his voice to a whisper, he said, "I made some friends at the Academy. When our frigate leaves for one of the central systems, I'm gonna jump ship and join the Alliance."

Luke was stunned. "The *Rebellion*?"

Biggs gripped Luke's arm. "Quiet down, will ya? You got a mouth bigger than a meteor crater!"

"I'm quiet, I'm quiet," Luke said, recovering fast

and lowering his voice to a rushed whisper. "Listen how quiet I am. You can barely hear me."

Biggs grinned and shook his head before he continued. "My friend has a friend on Bestine who might help us make contact."

"You're crazy," Luke said. "You could wander around forever trying to find them."

Biggs walked off with Luke in tow. "I know it's a long shot," Biggs said, raising his voice. "But if I don't find them, I'll do what I can on my own." Then he stopped to face his friend and said, "It's what we always talked about, Luke. I'm not going to wait around for the Empire to draft me into service. The Rebellion is spreading, and I want to be on the side I believe in."

"Yeah," Luke said. "Meanwhile, I'm stuck here." He started to shuffle off. Biggs followed.

"You'll get your chance to get off this rock," Biggs said. "You're going to the Academy next term, aren't you?"

"Not likely," Luke said. "I had to cancel my application."

"What for?"

"My uncle needs me."

Having heard that excuse too many times, Biggs groaned and rolled his eyes.

"No, I'm serious!" Luke said. "The Sand People

have been getting really crazy. They've even raided the outskirts of Anchorhead!"

"Come on, Luke," Biggs said. "Your uncle could hold off a whole colony of Sand People with one blaster."

Luke glowered. "I know. But we've almost got enough vaporators to make the place pay off. I have to stay one more season. I can't leave him now."

"What good's all your uncle's work if the Empire takes it over?" Biggs said. "You know they've already started to nationalize commerce in the central systems? It won't be long before your uncle's just a tenant, slaving for the greater glory of the Empire."

"No, that's not gonna happen here," Luke said. "You said yourself, the Empire won't even mess with this old rock."

"Things can change."

"I wish I *was* going," Luke said sullenly. "Are you going to be around long?"

Biggs shook his head. "No. I'm leaving in the morning."

"Then I guess I won't see you."

"Maybe someday," Biggs said. He clapped Luke on the back. "I'll keep a lookout."

"Yeah," Luke said. Then he brightened and said, "I'll be at the Academy soon enough . . . and then, who knows? I won't be drafted into the Imperial Starfleet, that's for sure." He extended his hand to Biggs. "Well, take it easy, buddy," he said as they shook hands. "You'll always be the best friend I've ever had."

"So long, Luke," Biggs said. Then he walked off, his cape flapping at his back.

Watching Biggs walk away, Luke wondered if it might indeed be the last time he'd ever see his friend. He also wondered if he really ever would make it off Tatooine.

The day after Luke witnessed the orbital space battle through his macrobinoculars, a group of Jawa merchants sold two droids to Owen Lars. One of the droids, an astromech unit named R2-D2, carried a secret message for someone named Obi-Wan Kenobi.

And Luke Skywalker's life was forever changed.

INTERLUDE

"*Excuse me, Master Luke,*" *C-3PO said as he and R2-D2 entered Luke's quarters on the* New Hope. "*Would you know where I might find Captain Solo? He told me to wait for him in the main galley. I waited, but... he never arrived. I'm afraid I can't find him anywhere.*"

"*I don't know why he wanted you to wait there,*" *Luke said,* "*but Han and Chewie are delivering supplies to some allies in the Outer Rim. They left in the* Falcon *over an hour ago.*"

"*Left!*" *C-3PO said indignantly.*

R2-D2 emitted a string of blurting beeps.

C-3PO glanced at the astromech beside him and said, "*You don't have to tell* me '*I told you so!*'" *The golden droid shook his head with dismay.* "*Sometimes, I get the distinct impression that Captain Solo deliberately misleads me. Come along, Artoo.*"

As the two droids made their exit, Luke grinned. Although he had come to regard C-3PO and R2-D2 as valued friends, he recalled that he hadn't been very impressed when he'd first met them on Tatooine. At the time, he'd been more interested in the prospect of getting some power converters at Tosche Station. But his view of them had changed when he'd learned of their escape from a Rebel Alliance ship, and then R2-D2 had projected a fragment of a holographic message from an imperiled princess.

Luke would never forget the swift series of events that had followed . . .

His reunion with Ben Kenobi in the Jundland Wastes, and his first awareness of the Force.

His horrific discovery of the charred remains of Owen and Beru, slain by Imperial stormtroopers who had been searching for the fugitive droids.

Meeting Han Solo and Chewbacca at Mos Eisley Spaceport, and escaping into space on the Millennium Falcon.

The realization that the Empire had obliterated the planet Alderaan.

The rescue of Princess Leia, and the death of Ben Kenobi on the Death Star.

The battle at Yavin, which had taken the lives of so many Rebel pilots, including Biggs Darklighter, shot down by Darth Vader in the Death Star's trench . . .

Over the course of just several fateful days, Luke had gained new allies and a sense of purpose. He had been transformed from a Tatooine farmboy into an enemy of the Empire and a hero of the Rebellion. But as he thought of Ben, Owen, Beru, and Biggs, he lowered his head sadly. He still had a hard time believing they were gone.

Granted, he hadn't entirely lost Ben. The Jedi had become one with the Force, and he endured as a spiritual entity who materialized infrequently. Although Luke could never predict when Ben's spirit might contact him, he sometimes sensed the Jedi's presence through the Force.

In the aftermath of the battle at Yavin, Luke had gone on several secret missions. On an assignment to infiltrate an Imperial base on Kalist VI, he was surprised to be reunited with his childhood friend Tank, who was by then a lieutenant in the Imperial Army. Although Tank had embraced the ideals of the Empire and attempted to turn Luke over to Darth Vader, he ultimately helped Luke save Leia during an Imperial attack.

While investigating a report of a new Imperial superweapon at the Starship Yards of Fondor, Luke met a lovely young woman, Tanith Shire, who worked as a supply-tug operator. The superweapon turned out to be an immense Star Destroyer that would eventually be used as Darth Vader's personal flagship, and Tanith helped Luke escape a trap that Vader had set for him. He and Tanith had parted with a kiss at a spaceport on the planet Kabal.

Once he'd returned to Yavin 4, Luke fought a hulking humanoid monster that he and other Rebels had come to call the Night Beast after it had made a series of nocturnal attacks. Impervious to blasterfire, the Night Beast turned out to be the long-dormant guardian of the Massassi, the original inhabitants of the ancient temple that the Alliance had transformed into their command headquarters. Fortunately, Luke had been able to use the Force to reach out and calm the creature. The Night Beast was placed on a Rebel transport so that it might deliver him to a reunion with the descendents of the Massassi.

Not long after that incident, a wounded Rebel agent returned from a mission to Aridus, which was how Luke had first learned of the desert planet that the New Hope *currently orbited. According to the agent, an old man wielding a lightsaber had saved him from a squad of stormtroopers, and his rescuer had identified himself as Ben Kenobi. C-3PO had traveled with Luke in a small smuggling ship to Aridus, where they'd soon discovered that "Kenobi" was really an actor hired by Darth Vader to lure Luke into yet another trap.*

Luke wondered, Was Vader trying to capture me because he sensed I was the pilot who destroyed the

Death Star, or did he know even then that I was his son? *Luke sighed. He doubted he would ever learn the answers to even half the questions he had about his father.*

Luke's quarters had a small viewport, and he gazed through it to see Aridus. He recalled how he and C-3PO had left the planet on their smuggling ship but almost immediately found themselves in unknown, and even more dangerous, territory. . . .

CHAPTER EIGHT

"We're in trouble, Threepio," Luke said, surveying the dead control console in their ship's cockpit. "Anything those Imperials we escaped *didn't* knock out, this crash has. No communicator, no power . . . no heat."

Luke and C-3PO had barely managed to flee Aridus in their ship before a squadron of Imperial TIE fighters sighted them and opened fire. Their ship had taken a severe pounding, but Luke had evaded the fighters by flying into the slipstream of a passing comet. The comet had carried them far across space at an incredible speed until it had entered a near collision course with an immense ice world in a star system that wasn't even on most galactic charts. The planet's gravitational pull had caused the comet to fragment before impact, but it had still taken all of Luke's piloting skills to make a crash landing.

Now the ship rested in a snow-filled valley beneath rocky cliffs. It was bad enough that Luke didn't know where they were and the engines were damaged beyond repair, but there wasn't any way to summon help either. He couldn't expect Princess Leia or anyone else at Rebel headquarters to find him. The other Rebels probably thought he was still on Aridus. They would never be able to trace his haphazard journey to the ice world.

He glanced out the viewport and saw a massive wall of dark clouds approaching over the frozen terrain. Stepping past C-3PO, he opened the ship's emergency locker and was relieved to find that it was stocked with insulated clothes and cold-weather survival equipment. C-3PO said, "Sir, my sensors indicate a steady and rapid decline in temperature. Night is approaching, I fear."

"More than night, Threepio," Luke said as pulled on a thermal jacket. "Look on the horizon. We've got a blizzard coming our way . . . fast."

C-3PO peered out the viewport while Luke tugged a snug hat over his head. Luke half expected the usually nervous droid to start trembling at the sight of the incoming storm, but C-3PO said in a reassuring tone, "Even wrecked, the ship is *some* shelter, Master Luke. Surely, with your thermal gear, you can weather whatever this dreadful ice world hurls at us."

"We'll find out soon, Threepio," Luke said. Although he had various regrets about his mission to Aridus, he had not been greatly bothered by the torrid climate that was so similar to Tatooine's. On the ice planet, warmth existed only as a memory.

He placed an emergency heat capsule in a small cylindrical furnace, set the device on the floor, and hunkered down beside it. Even with the thermal clothes on, he was colder than he'd ever been in his life.

"We could be much worse off, sir," C-3PO said, trying to sound cheery despite the storm that raged outside. "Suppose the comet had actually struck this miserable snowball of a world instead of narrowly missing it." Gazing out the viewport at the snow that had already almost completely covered their ship, he added, "And it's certainly the last place the Empire would look for anyone. Correct, Master Luke?"

C-3PO turned to face Luke, who remained seated beside the small furnace. Luke shivered as he stared at the furnace's dimming light. "Th-this is our last heat . . . emergency heat capsule," he stammered. "After it goes . . . don't know . . . h-how much longer . . . I'll be around, Threepio." Without knowing why, he lowered one trembling hand to his side to touch his lightsaber. He realized he felt some comfort just knowing that it was still clipped to his belt.

My father's lightsaber.

C-3PO was silent for a moment, then said, "The extreme cold must be playing havoc with my sensor circuitry. I could swear I detected something moving outside! Perhaps you should take a look, Master Luke . . . ?"

Luke slumped and collapsed on the floor beside the exhausted furnace.

He awoke to the sound of unfamiliar voices, and the smell and texture of oily fur against his face. He was still in his thermal clothes, his body draped over the body of a large creature. He didn't know how long he'd been unconscious or where he was, except that he was no longer in the ship.

He kept very still as he opened one eye. He saw that he was in some kind of ice cavern. It had a generator and other machinery in it. He could also see C-3PO standing beside a girl who wore a parka with a fur-lined hood, and also a man with a dark beard and thinning hair. The man wore a broad scarf around his neck and a gray tunic that was unmistakably an Imperial-issue officer's uniform. Luke guessed that the girl was near his own age. He kept his eye open and remained motionless as he listened to the man speak.

"You disobeyed me, Frija," the man said, "and jeopardized our safety! Fortunately, my experience as Imperial governor endows me with enough wisdom and resolve for both of us."

An Imperial governor? Luke wondered how and why the man had come to be so far from Imperial space.

The man drew a sleek blaster pistol from a holster at his belt, aimed the weapon at C-3PO, and said, "Droid, dump your injured master outside in the storm. Then report back for dismantling."

Before C-3PO could respond, the girl said, "Father, I won't let you harm this droid or his master! They've crashed on Hoth as we did. They're no threat!"

Hoth. Luke had never heard the planet's name before.

The girl moved closer to her father, placing her gloved hand on his wrist to make him lower the blaster. "I need the company of someone my own age! Someone young . . . attractive . . ."

"You're talking nonsense, Frija!" the man said as he yanked his wrist away, holding tight to the blaster. "Our survival depends on remaining alone! Trust me to eliminate this problem as an Imperial governor should!"

"Father, please!" Frija said. "I wasn't meant to be isolated and alone as we are here. I need friends . . . companionship . . ."

"I know what's best, Frija," the man said as he swung the blaster in Luke's direction. "Our safety cannot be imperiled for the sake of some half-frozen young fool!"

Luke had heard and seen enough. He swung his left leg up over the creature's back and then flung himself at the armed man. Luke caught the man around the neck and shoulders, but the man moved with surprising speed, bending fast to flip Luke onto the floor.

Luke gasped as he hit the floor. He realized he was still weak. As he began to push himself up, his attacker leveled the blaster at him.

"Your efforts gained you one thing, my overeager young troublemaker," the man said. "Death by blaster instead of being left to slowly freeze in Hoth's night storms."

But before the man could fire, Luke's arm swung up from his side with dazzling swiftness as his own weapon ignited. The blaster shattered in the man's grip.

The man looked dazed as his gaze traveled from his now-empty hand to Luke's weapon. "W-what?"

"A lightsaber," Luke said. "Weapon of the Jedi Knights. Funny . . . I'd think you were the right age to remember them." Keeping the lightsaber activated and his eyes fixed on the man's stunned face, Luke said, "Threepio, find their communicator and signal for help."

"You'll find that impossible, my young hero," the man said with a scowl. "You're stranded on Hoth."

"Pay no attention, Threepio. Just find their communicator. A few quick bleeps on our emergency signal frequency will bring help without alerting the Empire."

As Threepio tottered off toward a clustered array of technological equipment, the man glared at Luke and said, "Young fool. There's no danger of alerting *anyone.*"

A moment later, C-3PO stepped away from the equipment and said, "I've found their communicator, sir. Only, it's as hopelessly damaged as the one on our wrecked ship!"

Still facing the man, Luke said, "All your other equipment is okay. I think you've deliberately isolated yourself on Hoth."

The man sneered. "And you've joined us against my will."

Frija had pulled back her hood to reveal her face. Luke noticed that she had incredibly beautiful eyes, an icy blue that was strangely appropriate for their cold surroundings. He was surprised that she was so pretty, especially in contrast to her foul-tempered father. He deactivated his lightsaber but continued to watch the older man cautiously.

Looking at her father, Frija said, "He could have killed you and didn't. That proves he's not dangerous."

"His mere arrival has turned you against me, child," the man said sadly. "I deserted the Empire to save us, and letting mere loneliness attract you to this young fool is going to ruin that!" He threw an angry, defiant gaze at Luke.

Luke had noticed an enclosed cabin with a heavy metal door. He gestured to it and said, "Lock him up, Threepio. I've got an idea. . . ."

The next morning, the skies were clear as Luke and Frija left the cavernous hideout. They were mounted on a pair of tauntauns, reptomammals that were native to Hoth. Luke rode the same tauntaun that had carried him to the cave from his crashed ship. Frija had readily agreed to guide him back to his ship, although he had yet to explain the reason for their journey and why he had brought two empty saddle packs.

As the icy winds whipped at them, Luke said, "What were you doing away from your, uh, home when you found me and Threepio?"

"I was just out riding," Frija said. "I do that sometimes, just to get away for a while. Where you come from, did you ever just go riding?"

Luke recalled his old landspeeder as he squinted at the bright landscape. "Yeah, only it was warmer outside. A *lot* warmer." He smiled. "Frija, I'll never be able to fully thank you for saving me."

"I'm afraid I almost didn't. When I found your ship, I snuck up to it and looked through the window. I saw you lying on the floor. Your droid was trying to revive you. Naturally, I wanted to help, but then I thought of my father, and how he would react. And then . . . I climbed back on my tauntaun and I started to ride away."

"But you came back," Luke said. "Why?"

Frija's tauntaun made a grumbling sound, and she patted the side of the beast's neck. "Because I'm not my father," she said. "I couldn't let you die. I just couldn't."

Luke smiled at her. "You're very brave."

"That's kind of you to say," Frija said sadly. "But I'd be a liar if I said I didn't have a selfish interest in keeping you alive. Last night, I thought you were still unconscious up until you jumped off the tauntaun to stop my father, but . . . I guess you were awake, and you heard me, what I said about . . . needing someone young and attractive? To keep me company?"

Luke blushed. "Yeah," he said. "I did hear you say that."

"But I didn't mean that I needed just anyone," Frija said hastily. "I mean, I'm really, really glad I found *you*."

"Me too," Luke said, liking the girl more and more.

"There's your ship," Frija said, pointing to a distant gray spot in a wide white valley below their position. A fresh dusting of snow rested on the crashed vessel, which lay at an angle near a rocky outcropping.

As they rode down a hill toward the wreckage, Luke said, "Why didn't your father seek refuge with the Rebel Alliance, Frija?"

"He hates both sides."

Luke looked at Frija, expecting her to explain, but she didn't. Although he was curious about the reasons for her father's actions, he didn't want to upset Frija with too many questions.

A moment later, Frija interrupted the silence. "I'm sorry about our communicator, Luke. My father smashed it when we first arrived here."

Luke shook his head. "He's sure serious about isolating the two of you from the Empire *and* the Rebellion. But I think I've got a solution to the problem, especially since Threepio locked him away where he can't interfere."

As their tauntauns arrived at the crash site, Frija said, "Luke, I'm willing to defy my father to help you, except . . . what can we do here?"

"Yeah, my ship's communicator is as useless as yours," Luke said. "However, between the two, I bet we can cannibalize enough parts for a working model."

They dismounted the tauntauns and entered the ship. Once inside, Frija huddled beside Luke while he began disassembling the components he needed. Despite the freezing temperature, Luke could feel the warmth of Frija's breath against the side of his face.

It didn't take long for Luke to gather the necessary components. When he was finished, he said, "That does it, Frija. With the parts we've salvaged from this wreck's communicator, combined with the damaged one back at your cave, I'm sure I'll be signaling the Rebel Alliance in no time."

"It's wonderful working with you, Luke," Frija said. "Actually sharing some *purpose* . . . instead of just existing in isolation day after day as my father insists I do."

Frija helped carry the parts out to the tauntauns and load them into the saddle packs Luke had brought. "You don't know how happy I've been today," she said, "sharing your company, doing meaningful work."

"Hoth is a great place for hiding from the Empire, Frija," he said as he secured the packs, "but for a young girl like you to be isolated here is —"

A man's voice interrupted, "Her father's business! Which you've interfered with for the last time!"

Luke and Frija turned fast to see the renegade Imperial governor staring down at them from atop the nearby outcropping. The governor held a blaster rifle.

Luke had no idea how the governor had escaped from the base. He hoped that C-3PO was undamaged.

"Father, leave us alone!" Frija cried. "I'm happy helping Luke!"

"He'll soon bring his Rebel friends swarming, Frija, and the Imperials won't be far behind. The war I deserted the Empire to *save* us from will be right here on Hoth! You'll thank me for this later, child."

The governor aimed his rifle at Luke, who was standing within arm's reach of Frija. At the same moment the governor squeezed the trigger, Frija threw her body against Luke's and shouted, "No!"

The energy beam crashed into the ground near the feet of the two tumbling figures, and the explosive noise echoed through the valley. Luke rolled quickly to his feet and pulled Frija up from the snow.

"Frija! You almost took that blast meant for me!"

"I won't let him hurt you, Luke!" Frija said. "He won't dare shoot again if I'm right beside you!"

"I can't take that chance," Luke said. He pointed to the tauntauns. "Get out of here, Frija. I don't know where the governor got that blaster, but it's me he wants, not you. I can handle him."

Frija hesitated for just a moment. Then she grabbed the reins for Luke's tauntaun and jumped up onto the back of her own.

The governor said, "I've weapons hidden in every compartment of our ice cave, Skywalker. That's how I blasted my way out of confinement! I knew the day would come when Rebels or Imperials would threaten our safety here." He took aim and fired again.

Luke leaped aside as the next energy beam slammed into the icy ground. As the governor prepared to fire once more, Luke looked at Frija and the tauntauns, who hadn't budged. "He's berserk!" Luke said. "Get those communicator parts to Threepio! I'll draw your father's fire!"

Hearing this, the governor said, "Communicator parts!"

Frija dug her boots into her tauntaun's sides while she tugged the reins for the other tauntaun. Just as the beasts began moving away from Luke and the wrecked ship, another blaster shot rang out.

The blast caught Frija in the back. She fell from her mount and collapsed against the snow.

Luke gasped.

The governor lowered his rifle. "Frija!" he cried. "No! I wanted to hit the pack with the communicator parts!"

Luke was outraged. He was already running for the governor as he drew and ignited his lightsaber. The governor heard the lightsaber's energized hum and turned to see Luke's approach. Glaring at the governor, Luke said bitterly, "You wanted to keep her cut off on this planet so badly you killed her!"

"It's *your* fault my daughter turned against me!" the governor snapped. "It's your fault I had to shoot her . . . and now you'll die for it!" He raised his rifle.

Luke had no choice but to swing his lightsaber. Its blade met the rifle's barrel just as the governor squeezed the trigger. The rifle jerked as it backfired a split second before the lightsaber swept through the sleeve of the governor's tunic and across the back of his right hand.

The governor collapsed in the snow and lay motionless.

Luke stood over the governor's body. He hadn't meant to cut the man down, only disable his rifle. Luke was amazed that he had somehow avoided the rifle's blast, but he was even more stunned by what he saw through the torn fabric across the governor's chest.

Wires?

Luke bent down beside the lifeless form. The governor's open wound exposed not only wires but other mechanical components. Luke noticed that a layer of synthetic flesh had peeled away from the back of the governor's right hand to reveal bare metal fingers and joints.

He's . . . an elaborate sort of droid!

"Luke?"

It was Frija, calling weakly from where she'd fallen. Both tauntauns remained standing a short distance from her.

Leaving the governor's body, Luke ran through the snow until he arrived at the girl's side. As he knelt down next to her, he saw that one of her hands was also an exposed tangle of wires and robotic metal fingers.

Frija was trying to push herself up from the ground. Luke's eyes met her ice blue gaze. At first he wasn't sure what to say. Then he saw her lower lip tremble.

"Frija," he said. "I never meant for anything to happen to you or your father."

"Don't blame yourself, Luke!" Frija said. "We're both mechanical . . . created by Imperial technicians." She coughed, exhaling steam into the frigid air.

Luke eased his arm under her back to elevate her head and shoulders. As he held her close against him, she continued, "We were designed to be decoys . . . programmed to imitate the *real* governor and his daughter so they could flee a Rebel attack." She lifted her eyebrows. "Perhaps we were programmed too perfectly. My father's survival instincts were so strong he had us escape instead." She coughed again. "The Empire designed my father and me to be *targets* for the Rebels. That's why he hated both sides."

Luke shook his head. "If I hadn't crashed here, Frija, the two of you would be living safely and happily."

"No," Frija said. "Merely existing. And we weren't created to last long." She raised her hand and pressed her robotic fingers against the sleeve of Luke's jacket.

Luke reached for her hand and held it in his own.

"You brought purpose and enjoyment to the time I had," Frija said. "Don't regret what happened here, Luke. I thank you for it."

She coughed again, and Luke felt her hand go slack.

"Rebuild the communicator," Frija said, "and summon your friends. I'm sorry my father fought so against you . . . but I'm glad you came to Hoth."

"For the chance to have known you, Frija, so am I . . . so am I."

Frija closed her eyes, and her head tilted back.

Luke just sat there for a moment, holding Frija. He almost didn't notice the snowflakes that had begun to fall from the darkening sky. And then he heard C-3PO calling to him.

Although C-3PO had been unable to prevent the governor from escaping the cave, he had followed the tracks through the snow until he arrived at the crash site. Greatly relieved to find Luke unharmed, he listened with interest as Luke told him that Frija and her father had been mechanical beings, and then explained why her father had been so angered by Luke's arrival.

When Luke was finished, C-3PO said, "Fortunately, Frija didn't share her father's hatreds, sir. She seemed *particularly* happy with you."

"Thanks to her, we'll leave Hoth soon, Threepio," Luke said. He lifted Frija's body carefully from the ground.

C-3PO noticed Frija's exposed robotic hand. "Most remarkable," he said. "I believe the Alliance scientists will be quite interested in learning about this human replica droid."

"But they won't," Luke said. He turned his head so the golden droid wouldn't see his grief-stricken expression. "I'm going to bury her. And her father."

After Luke and C-3PO returned with the tauntauns to the ice cave, Luke had no difficulty patching together a makeshift communicator. He quickly notified the

Alliance of his whereabouts and proposed that they relocate their headquarters to the remote ice world. Soon he was reunited with his friends, and the Alliance Corps of Engineers went to work, expanding the original ice cave and creating many larger ones.

He had no need to tell the engineers about the two graves near his crash site, an area already covered by a fresh, heavy layer of snow. And although he could only ever imagine why his uncle had removed the headstones from the family plot on Tatooine, he realized that he cherished his memories of Frija more than he felt compelled to leave a monument on Hoth that would eventually give way to time.

He left both graves unmarked.

CHAPTER NINE

"Help!" a woman screamed from across the forest. "Please! Someone! Help!"

Luke was surprised to hear any stranger's voice. Because the *Millennium Falcon*'s sensors had not detected any evidence of civilization on the jungle planet, he hadn't expected to encounter any intelligent life forms. Without hesitation, he turned and bolted through dense foliage, running toward the unseen woman.

Luke, Han Solo, Chewbacca, C-3PO, and R2-D2 had been on the *Falcon*, traveling with the Rebel fleet after hastily evacuating their former base on Yavin 4. They had guided the fleet to a hyperspace jump point that would take them directly to their new base on the ice planet Hoth. Unfortunately, when they had attempted to follow the other ships through hyperspace, the *Falcon*'s navigational computer had gone haywire. The *Falcon* had emerged from hyperspace in an unknown sector, and the crew had been forced to land on the uncharted world to make repairs to the navicomputer as well as the hyperdrive.

Han had been anxious about the planet even before they'd landed. He maintained that trouble always had a way of finding them on apparently peaceful worlds, and he had encouraged Luke to scout around to make sure that nothing unpleasant would interrupt their work on the *Falcon*. Initially, all Luke had found were strangely beautiful plants, towering trees, and a few small non-threatening creatures. He had been musing that Han's anxiety was unfounded — before the woman's scream pierced the tranquil forest.

Luke vaulted over a thick, fungus-covered root of an enormous tree to arrive at the edge of a clearing. He found himself facing a monstrous plant with an eyeless, bulbous head and a gaping maw. Long tentacle-like tendrils extended from beneath the head, and one tendril was coiled around a terrified girl. She had fair skin and blond hair, and her scant clothing appeared to be made from animal skins. To Luke's astonishment, he recognized her.

Tanith Shire?

He hadn't seen Tanith since they'd gone their separate ways at a spaceport on the planet Kabal, where they'd parted with a kiss. She'd been wearing more conventional clothes at the time.

Luke ignited his lightsaber and rushed the carnivorous plant. His blade swept through one tendril, but then another appendage lashed out and struck his wrist so hard that the lightsaber was knocked from his grasp. As the lightsaber fell to the forest floor, Luke found himself suddenly lifted off his feet by the powerful monster.

The tendrils snaked and constricted around Luke's body. He managed to extend his right hand over the grip of his holstered blaster pistol, but the monster pinned his arms to his sides. Desperate to reach his blaster, he extended his fingers as far as he could.

Luke still had much to learn about the power of the Force. He wasn't even trying to use the Force when the pistol sailed out of its holster into his waiting grip. As the monster twisted and tightened its hold on him, Luke squeezed the blaster's trigger.

He shot the monster at point-blank range. It let out a rasping shriek, and then all of its tendrils went slack. Luke rolled away from the creature. As he pushed himself up from the ground, he was surprised to see Tanith running off into the forest.

"Tanith!" Luke called out. "What are you doing? Come back!" But she did not pause. Wondering if the girl was in shock or required medical attention, Luke recovered his lightsaber, holstered his blaster, and then ran after her.

Luke wondered how Tanith had wound up on the jungle planet. He couldn't understand why she was running away from him. *Doesn't she recognize me?*

"Tanith!"

Broad-leaved plants whipped at Luke as he raced through the jungle. He'd lost sight of Tanith in the shadows of the surrounding growth. Ducking under the fleshy, umbrella-shaped cap of a tall fungus, he suddenly spotted her again. She was running straight for the ledge of a high cliff.

"No!" Luke yelled as he sprinted after the girl. She stopped short at the edge and turned, allowing Luke to see her frightened face. Luke leaped forward, grabbing her arm in an effort to haul her back from the edge, but then she lost her footing and fell backward, pulling Luke with her.

They fell and plunged into the water of a deep, swiftly moving river. Having grown up on Tatooine, Luke was an inexperienced swimmer and had to fight his way to the surface. He saw Tanith flailing ahead of him, her wet hair plastered over her face. As the river carried them downstream, Luke struggled over to her side and caught her by the arm.

"Tanith! Hang on! I've got you!" He pulled her toward the shore until he found his footing in the shallows. When they reached the river's edge, he finally got a good, close look at the girl's face. Although her eyes were filled with fear, he could see she was very beautiful.

But she wasn't the girl he remembered.

"You're not Tanith Shire," Luke said in a daze as he followed the girl up onto the mucky shore. She backed away from him, cringing. She had long dark hair and a lean face with grayish blue eyes that Luke found strangely haunting. He couldn't understand why his own eyes had deceived him earlier, not just when he'd first seen her, but right up until the moment they'd fallen into the stream.

The girl continued to look at Luke with apprehension. Luke felt slightly dizzy as he faced her from the stream's edge. "What's going on around here?" he asked. "Who are you? What made me think you were Tanith Shire? You don't look similar at all."

"I am S'ybll," the girl said, her voice trembling. "I fear the atmosphere of my world is sometimes too rich. For strangers, almost intoxicating. It is easy to imagine things. . . ."

"It's sure got me confused," Luke said. He looked away from the girl to survey the jungle. "If I mistook you for someone totally different, how much else have I imagined? Wondering all the time if what I see is real or not could turn into quite a . . . problem!"

Luke's wandering gaze had landed on an Imperial stormtrooper who stood just a short distance away, in the shadow of a tall tree. The white-armored trooper held a blaster rifle that was leveled in the direction of Luke and the unarmed girl.

Luke moved without thinking, pulling his lightsaber from his belt and igniting its energy beam as he leaped at the trooper. The trooper didn't flinch as Luke swung his lightsaber hard and fast through the plastoid armor. Luke was surprised when the shattered armor instantly fell away to reveal that it had been stuffed with bundled sticks. The armor and sticks collapsed with a loud clatter.

Luke looked down at the heap that rested at his feet. "S'ybll? This is just an empty suit of stormtrooper armor. Why . . . ?"

"I placed it here, Luke, in hopes it might keep intruders at bay," S'ybll said as she stepped past the armor. "My home is just ahead."

Did she just say my name? Luke didn't remember whether he'd introduced himself to S'ybll, but decided he must have. "Intruders?" he said as he followed her. "What kind of intruders?"

"My planet appears to be a tropical paradise, but there are dangers . . . wild beasts and such."

"But empty stormtrooper armor frightens them off?" Luke asked skeptically.

"Sometimes," S'ybll said. "Perhaps it is foolish. Still . . . it is not easy for a woman alone to defend her home." She gestured to the ruins of an ancient structure that rose from the jungle floor. The structure included a flight of stone steps that led up to a series of architectural columns, some of which were still standing and supported broad lintels. Other columns lay broken. While a number appeared to have fallen, possibly because of erosion over many centuries, a few looked like they'd been deliberately toppled.

Gazing at the timeworn structure, Luke was reminded of the abandoned base on Yavin 4. Then his stomach clenched as he noticed several more propped-up suits of stormtrooper armor. He said, "This is your home, S'ybll?"

"You find it strange I use a ruin as my home?"

"No, S'ybll. Coincidental. Until recently, Rebel Alliance headquarters were in something similar." As soon as the words were out of his mouth, Luke realized that he couldn't remember if he'd mentioned his affiliation with the Alliance to S'ybll. He rubbed his eyes, then gestured to the empty suits of armor. "What I *do* find strange is all this stormtrooper armor . . . and no stormtroopers. What happened to the men inside?"

"I told you my planet is not quite the paradise it appears, Luke," S'ybll said as she directed Luke to a clearing beside the ruins. "These Imperials came exploring, and learned just how dangerous this world can be."

In the clearing rested an Imperial *Lambda*-class shuttle. Covered by thick moss and fungal growth, the vessel's exterior was heavily battered. However, its wings were raised, and both the landing gear and the ramp were fully deployed.

"The damage to this shuttle didn't come from a crash, S'ybll." Luke pointed to the cockpit's shattered transparisteel canopy. "This hole was made from the outside. It'd take something pretty terrible to inflict it." He turned to S'ybll and was taken aback by the concerned look on her face. Hoping to make light of his comment, he said, "First, empty suits of stormtrooper armor to give me a scare . . . now a smashed Imperial shuttle! You've got weird taste in home decoration, S'ybll."

"This craft landed *long* before I settled in this ruin, Luke Skywalker," S'ybll said testily. "Whatever happened to those soldiers, I merely propped their armor about to frighten off wild creatures."

Luke gulped. "I was only joking, S'ybll," he said. "Didn't mean to insult your defenses. But I doubt they'll stop anything that could damage a ship this way."

Unexpectedly, S'ybll moved close to Luke and wrapped her arms around his shoulders. "My planet is full of such dangers, Luke. I need someone to protect me. Someone like *you*."

Luke was surprised by S'ybll's behavior but did not try to move away from her. As she tilted her chin toward the derelict Imperial shuttle, she said, "You *see* the damage done to this ship of the Empire,

Luke. Suppose whatever inflicted it returns? I need protection."

"But, S'ybll . . ."

"I need you," she whispered before she pulled him closer and kissed him.

Luke backed away. "S'ybll . . . please," he said. "I'll do what I can to help you. But . . . I have other commitments. To my friends. To the Rebel Alliance . . . and to . . ."

S'ybll's eyes suddenly brimmed with tears. Before he could ask her what was wrong, she turned away from him and ran from the shuttle, heading into the ruins.

Flabbergasted, Luke stood beside the shuttle for a moment, then looked off in the direction that S'ybll had fled. Only then did he notice that night had begun to fall. "S'ybll!" he shouted. "Where did you run to? I didn't mean to upset you, but I can't just desert my friends here and —"

Luke saw a shadowy form pass behind one of the old columns. At first he thought it was S'ybll, but a moment later, the hulking form emerged from the ruins to reveal itself.

It was a humanoid creature, nearly three meters tall, with green skin, long arms, and a massive torso. It had fangs and reptilian eyes. Luke recognized the monster instantly. It was either the Night Beast — the creature he'd previously encountered on Yavin 4 — or its identical twin.

The monster growled, then sprang at Luke. Luke leaped away and started running. He tried to reach out to the beast with his mind but could not sense any connection. Glancing back over his shoulder, he saw the monster lift a large block of stone and hurl it.

Luke vaulted over a fallen column to avoid being hit by the flying block. The block smashed into the column. Luke kept running. He considered reaching for his blaster but decided against it. Not just because he recalled that energy weapons had little effect on the Night Beast, but because he didn't know where S'ybll was hiding, and he was afraid an indiscriminate blast might cause a cave-in.

"S'ybll!" Luke shouted as he ran. "Where are you?"

The monster was catching up with him. Despite its incredible resemblance to the Night Beast, Luke was practically certain it wasn't the same creature that had left Yavin 4 on a transport ship. The possibility of finding the Night Beast on such a far-flung world, and so shortly after their last encounter on Yavin 4 . . . Luke couldn't begin to calculate the odds.

Remembering his comlink, Luke decided to summon help from Han and Chewie. Still running, he reached to his belt.

His comlink was gone.

Must've lost it when S'ybll and I fell into the river!

The monster picked up another massive stone and hurled it. The stone crashed into the ground right in front of Luke.

Luke stumbled over the stone and sprinted around the ruins. Arriving at a high, rough wall that was part of the structure's foundation, he jumped up and began scaling it. He expected the monster to follow, and he planned on having his lightsaber ready. But as he gripped a chunk of stone and began to pull himself up, the ancient stone crumbled.

"No!" he shouted as he fell backward through the air. He thought the monster was just below his position and that he'd fall right into its arms. Instead, he hit the ground hard. His back and legs took most of the impact but did nothing to stop the back of his head from striking the ground too.

He lay on the ground, the wind knocked out of him. Forcing his eyes open, he saw that the sky overhead was now a deep, dark blue.

He moaned as he rolled over and rubbed the back of his head. As best as he could tell, he hadn't broken any bones, but just about everything hurt.

And then he remembered the monster. He knew he had to get up fast, before it —

"Luke."

It was a man's voice. Still dazed and sprawled on the ground, Luke turned his head and saw the silhouette of a robed figure standing a short distance away, in the shadow of a still-standing column. Luke's eyes flicked around as he searched for the monster.

"The danger is past, my boy," the robed man said, "but I'm concerned for your new companion." The man moved out from the darkness.

He was Ben Kenobi.

"Ben?" Luke gasped. "How . . . ?"

"I'm always with you, young Luke," Ben said. "And it seems my sudden appearance has driven away the creature which menaced you. But what of your new companion, and the dangers which menace her?"

New companion? It took a moment for Luke to realize whom Ben was talking about. He said, "S'ybll?"

Ben nodded.

"Ben . . . I'm still groggy from my fall." Luke struggled to his feet and looked around anxiously. "How did a monster from my past appear here? Where did it go?"

"There are many monsters here, Luke," Ben said with a shrug, "even on a planetary paradise such as this. That is why your new friend, S'ybll, needs you, my boy. That is why you *must* go to her."

Luke clutched his head. "Han . . . the droids . . . Chewbacca . . . They're all waiting for me, Ben."

"There will be time for them later, my boy. For now, it's S'ybll you must consider. Go to her."

"She hid before the monster appeared," Luke said

absently as he staggered toward Ben. Glancing up at the ruins, he continued, "Was it here, Ben? You want me . . . to go here?"

But Ben had vanished.

"Help me," Luke said. "I feel . . . so . . . so weak." His legs buckled and he fell forward onto the ground.

"B-Ben?"

Luke tried opening his eyes but he saw nothing. Nothing at all. Somehow he had been engulfed by darkness.

His mouth was dry and his entire body ached. Shifting his legs and elbows slightly, he realized he was lying flat on his back against a hard surface.

"I must've blacked out," he muttered aloud. "Where are you, Ben?"

But it wasn't Ben who answered. It was S'ybll.

"Your friend is gone, Luke," she said. "But all is fine. He convinced you not to leave but to join me here . . . here in my hiding place."

Luke felt her fingers push through his hair. "S'ybll?" he said. "There's something over my eyes . . . ?"

"Just a damp cloth, Luke. Don't touch it. You suffered a slight concussion from your fall. Just relax. Let me treat you."

Her voice sounded so tranquil, comforting . . .

Luke felt a supple pressure against his cheek, and then S'ybll's hair brushed against his face. He felt her take his right hand in hers, and she began massaging his fingers.

"Funny, S'ybll," Luke mumbled deliriously. "Ben Kenobi appeared to me . . . wanted me to find you . . . help you. But really . . . you're helping *me*."

"Just relax."

"I felt like . . . you were kissing me earlier."

"Lie still," S'ybll said soothingly. "I know what I'm doing. I've done this many times before."

Luke smelled something burning. Candles. Maybe dried leaves too. He cleared his throat. "S'ybll, is it still night? You've stayed with me for so long."

"I like being close to you, Luke."

"Didn't think the fall hurt me much," he said. "But . . . keep feeling weaker."

"Just relax," S'ybll repeated. "Let me treat you. It's best if you have quiet."

And then, unexpectedly, Luke heard C-3PO's voice. "Master Luke? Master Luke!" the droid said. "Are you there, sir? Come in . . . please!"

Luke was suddenly alert. He tried to push himself up from the flat surface he'd been resting on, and drew one hand toward his face.

"Lie still," S'ybll said. "Don't move. Don't take the cloth from your eyes."

"S'ybll," Luke said, pushing against her shoulder. "That voice. It was one of my droids . . . Threepio!"

And then C-3PO spoke again. "Artoo-Detoo, I feel

126

most silly doing this. If Master Luke lost his comlink, he can't possibly hear us!"

"My comlink!" Luke said. He sat up fast, pulling the damp cloth from his face as he turned his head in the direction of C-3PO's voice. He was in a gloomy chamber and had been resting on some kind of altar. Smoke was rising from an archaic urn as well as from several candles. A stone table was placed near the altar. On the table were his lightsaber, blaster pistol, and comlink.

Luke stared at the comlink. "S'ybll . . . I thought it fell off . . . when we plunged into the river from the cliff. The only way it could've gotten here is if you . . ."

S'ybll pushed Luke aside and snatched up the comlink. Only then did he see her face.

Although she remained attired in the animal skins, the woman who stood before him was a wretched, withered figure, with filthy white hair and deathly pale, wrinkled flesh that was broken with many warts. Spittle flew from her yellow teeth as she snapped, "I *told* you not to take the cloth from your eyes!"

Luke felt light-headed. He blinked as he tried to determine what was real and what wasn't. "You stole my comlink, S'ybll. . . . Hid it here . . . in your quarters. . . ."

"Yes, Luke," S'ybll said, her voice a low rasp. "Right off your equipment belt. I wanted to use it later, to lure your friends to these ruins after I was through with you."

Luke shook his head. "S'ybll, what's happened to you?"

"You're seeing me as I *am*, Luke. I've always looked this way. Until visitors like you — and an Imperial exploration team before you — arrived to help me. As your friends will arrive . . . following your comlink." She extended a bony arm to place the comlink on the altar. "It might be difficult dealing with all of you at once, but by the time they're here, I'll be done with you."

Luke backed up cautiously toward the stone table.

"Stand still, Luke," S'ybll said. "You're too weak. Too under my spell to escape now!"

"D-don't know what you've done to me," he stammered as he grabbed his weapons from the table. "But I won't just give up!" He scanned the chamber and sighted a curving flight of stone steps that appeared to be the only exit. Dim light shone down from the top of the stairwell.

"Yes," S'ybll hissed as Luke secured the weapons to his belt. "There's great power in you. I sensed that. It's what attracted me. But it's mostly unformed . . . you've not yet mastered it. And now you never will!" She lurched forward and threw her arms around him.

Luke gasped. His arms flexed away from his body against his will. He wanted to break away from S'ybll and reach for his weapons, but he couldn't budge.

"Don't fight, Luke. Just give in to my embrace. The pain won't last long."

Her breath was awful. Luke tried to pull himself away from S'ybll, but her arms remained locked around him. As his senses reeled, he thought, *Who . . . what are you?*

"I'm a mind witch," S'ybll said. "I was ancient when these ruins were new. I can reach into your memories and create illusions to ensnare and weaken you until a psychic link is forged. Then I drain the mental energy from you, the very life essence that will renew me . . . make me young again! Just as I drained the energy of the Imperial soldiers . . ."

Luke closed his eyes and struggled to concentrate. He felt S'ybll probing his mind. He thought, *Get out!*

"There's no resisting, Luke. You'll soon be an empty husk. It's too late . . . even with the Force running so richly within your being."

She knows about the Force!

"The hold of the mind witch is upon you. Give in!"

"*No!*" Luke shouted as he opened his eyes and flung his arms out, launching S'ybll away from him and sending her to the floor. It took all his concentration to turn for the stone steps. Ignoring a human skull that had been transformed into a candle holder, he began climbing.

As he ascended from the subterranean lair, Luke heard S'ybll's cackle travel up the stairway. "You're strong!" she said. "So much stronger than I suspected. But you're too weak to run far. And with the psychic links I've forged, your very thoughts . . . your greatest fears . . . are mine to use against you!"

Luke saw the exit ahead of him. It was daybreak, and a heavy layer of mist hung in the morning air. S'ybll cackled again, and Luke could still hear her dreadful laughter echoing off the stairwell's walls as he emerged outside, amid the columnar ruins.

Darth Vader was waiting for him. Looming beside a massive column, the Dark Lord of the Sith extended the red blade of his lightsaber and said, "I have you at last, young Skywalker."

Vader swept toward him. Luke cringed and nearly stumbled back into the stairwell. He had no intention of falling into S'ybll's clutches again. Keeping his eyes on Vader, he edged away from the stairwell but acciden- tally backed into a column.

Vader swung his blade at Luke's head. Luke ducked and the lightsaber flashed over him, striking the column. The impact made a loud crack, and as Luke leaped aside and looked back, he saw what appeared to be a fresh gouge across the column's face.

Luke knew that Vader was just an illusion created by the mind witch, but . . . *It seems so real!*

Out of the corner of his eye, Luke saw S'ybll emerge from the stairwell just as Vader advanced toward him again. Luke realized that there was only one way to resist.

I've got to stop and be calm.

Instead of staring at the illusion of Vader, he relaxed and stared through it.

Vader stopped in front of Luke, raised the lightsaber, and swung hard. The red blade appeared to pass directly through Luke's body, but it had absolutely no effect on him. Luke stood his ground as Vader swung again.

"Your illusions are frightening, S'ybll," Luke said as the image faded and vanished. "But the only way they can do real harm is if I give in to them."

"I've underestimated you," S'ybll said bitterly. "Now you force me to demonstrate that a mind witch's powers extend far beyond weaving illusions!" She clenched a bony fist at Luke. "I can wield physical objects!"

Luke heard a loud breaking noise to his left, and he looked up to see that two neighboring columns had suddenly broken in half and were swaying toward him, along with the massive lintel they had supported for ages. Luke sensed it was no illusion.

S'ybll said, "I hate to crush a source of mental energies which can feed and renew me, but your friends should arrive soon to replace you!"

Luke instinctively calculated the trajectory of the falling stones and jumped just before they came crashing down where he'd been standing. He moved faster than S'ybll could keep track of him, and jumped over and behind a fragment of a broken lintel. Dust and debris flew in all directions.

The cloud of dust was still settling when Luke heard a welcome voice call out from the jungle. "Luke? Luke! It's Han and Chewie! You around, kid? What was that crash we heard?"

"This way!" S'ybll replied. "Hurry! Please! Your friend's been hurt!"

Emerging from the rubble, Luke said, "Not as fatally as you think, S'ybll. You've weakened me, but not so much I couldn't dodge one falling rock."

The mind witch glared at him. "You dare taunt me? Perhaps you need a final demonstration of just how far a mind witch's ability to move physical objects can go!" She lifted her arms and gestured at the ruins.

A sound like rolling thunder rippled across the area, and then the ruins exploded. Heavy stones rained down, smashing all around Luke. He suddenly felt as if he were trying to escape a meteor shower, but he also saw an opportunity to use S'ybll's powers against her. He ran fast to dodge the debris, then turned and ran back toward S'ybll.

S'ybll sneered at him as he changed course. He saw her try to redirect a large stone through the air in his direction, and he also saw a column that was falling toward her.

The stones crashed into the ground. The noise was followed by an almost total silence.

Luke stepped out from the rubble. A moment later, he saw Han and Chewbacca arrive at the edge of the ruins.

"Luke!" Han shouted. "Chewie, the droids, and I have been been blasted worried! What happened here, kid?"

"I made someone very angry, Han." Luke gestured at one of the toppled columns. A pale, bony arm jutted out from underneath it. "A mind witch," Luke continued. "She meant to kill me and renew herself by draining you two of your mental energies. I gambled that if she got enraged enough, the effort would exhaust her own energies instead. And without anything to sustain her, she collapsed as she should have ages ago."

Han glanced at Chewbacca and said, "I've heard of mind witches. Always thought they were just a crazy myth."

Luke said, "I guess S'ybll was the last of her kind."

"Since she intended to leave us like she wound up herself, I sure hope so! Time we left this paradise, kid."

They left the ruins and made their way back through the jungle to the *Millennium Falcon*. Although the *Falcon*'s navicomputer remained temperamental, they managed to get back to Hoth and rejoin their allies at Echo Base.

*　　*　　*

Three years had passed since the destruction of the Death Star at Yavin 4, but the days were numbered for the Rebellion's new secret headquarters. Not long after the *Falcon*'s return to the ice planet, an Imperial probe droid arrived on Hoth and subsequently transmitted an image of the Rebel base's large power generator back to the Imperial fleet.

And then the Empire struck back.

As Luke reflected on his encounter with the mind witch, he recalled that it hadn't been the first time he'd confronted an apparition of Darth Vader. Not long after he'd destroyed the Death Star, he'd been recovering from an ill-fated meditation exercise when he'd dreamed of a duel with Vader. Ben Kenobi had appeared in the dream too, and when Luke awakened, it was with the certainty that Vader had survived the Battle of Yavin. Later, after the Battle of Hoth, he had faced yet another phantom, in a cave while he'd trained with the Jedi Master Yoda on the swamp planet Dagobah.

Luke had also had very real confrontations with Darth Vader on Monastery and Circarpous V — but all those experiences paled compared with his duel with Vader at Bespin, in Cloud City's reactor shaft. . . .

CHAPTER TEN

Darth Vader's lightsaber swept through Luke's wrist.

Luke screamed. His hand arced away from the suddenly cauterized stub at the end of his right arm, carrying his lightsaber with it. The lightsaber automatically deactivated, and the weapon fell with the severed hand, like inconsequential refuse, into the incredibly deep reactor shaft.

Luke was balanced on a metal beam that jutted out from a long gantry in the shaft. Vader stood looming at the gantry's outer edge, just above Luke's position. The reactor's high winds whipped hard at both men. Luke clutched his wounded arm to his chest and slumped down on the beam.

"There is no escape," Vader said as Luke struggled to move away from him, crawling backward on the beam. "Don't make me destroy you, Luke."

But Luke kept crawling. He felt dizzy and sick. His only goal was to put distance between himself and Vader.

The Sith Lord switched off his lightsaber. "You do not yet realize your importance," he continued. "You have only begun to discover your power. Join me and I will complete your training. With our combined strength, we can end this destructive conflict and bring *order* to the galaxy."

Luke reached the end of the beam and wrapped his arms around a sensor array. Below him, there was a ring of metal, and beyond that, nothing but the yawning shaft. He turned to face Vader. "I'll never join you!"

"If only you knew the power of the dark side," Vader said. He reached out to clutch the air with his black-gloved fist. "Obi-Wan never told you what happened to your father."

"He told me enough!" Luke lowered his feet to the metal ring. Wincing, he added, "He told me you killed him."

"No," Vader said, his fist still clenched. "I am your father."

Luke's eyes opened wide. *My father? But Ben told me . . .* "No," Luke whimpered. "No. That's not true! That's impossible!"

"Search your feelings," Vader said. "You know it to be true."

"No!" Luke shouted. "No!"

The wind picked up, and Vader's black cape rippled at his back. "Luke — you can destroy the Emperor. He has foreseen this. It is your destiny." He opened his left hand and held it out to Luke. "Join me, and together we can rule the galaxy as father and son."

His voice is so hypnotic, Luke thought, and he felt part of him falling under Vader's spell. But only part. He looked into the shaft that seemed to stretch down to forever.

"Come with me," Vader urged. "It is the only way."

Luke stared up at Vader and felt a certain calmness as he thought, *No. It's not the only way.*

He released his arms from the sensor array and fell, down, down into the reactor shaft. There was nothing to break his fall. As he tumbled through the air, he looked up, half expecting to see Vader leaping down after him. But all he saw of Vader was a rapidly receding black speck at the edge of the already distant gantry.

INTERLUDE

Sitting in front of a computer console in his quarters on the New Hope, Luke extended the fingers of his right hand and flexed them. Few people would ever guess that the hand was a cybernetic prosthetic. The surgeon droid on the Rebel medical frigate had done a superb job of replicating his hand, right down to the fingerprints. And thanks to Ben Kenobi, who'd written a book that Luke discovered in Ben's home on Tatooine, Luke had been able to construct a new lightsaber. Following Ben's written instructions, Luke had modified his weapon with flasback waterseals so it wouldn't short-circuit if it made contact with water, as his first lightsaber had done when he was on Mimban.

As Luke recalled the encounter with Vader on Cloud City, he didn't feel angry about his father's actions. Darth Vader had been the Emperor's servant, and the dark side had consumed nearly every trace of goodness in him. But in the end, on the second Death Star, at the Battle of Endor, the goodness that remained in Luke's father won out over the dark side. Anakin Skywalker destroyed the Sith, and he died a Jedi.

Luke wished Leia could see it that way too.

Granted, he could understand her bitterness. Not only had Vader committed scores of atrocities, but some of his nefarious schemes had survived the death of Anakin Skywalker. Luke thought of Shira Brie, the Force-sensitive Imperial agent who had infiltrated the Rebel Alliance. Although the Rebels had been led to believe that Shira had been killed during a mission, Vader had had her shattered body rebuilt and transformed her into his protégée. Recently, Shira had reemerged as Lumiya, the self-proclaimed Dark Lady of the Sith. Her present whereabouts were unknown.

Luke returned his attention to the computer console. He was using the computer to search the holonet for any and all data about the Jedi Order. Unfortunately, most of the information he found was merely old Imperial propaganda. The Empire's leaders still claimed that the Jedi Knights who had served the Republic during the Clone Wars had been secretly plotting to overthrow the Republic and conquer the galaxy. Luke knew that the data was rubbish, and that it was the Emperor who had manipulated events to bring down the Jedi Order and fulfill his own ambitions.

Luke didn't expect to find any data about Obi-Wan Kenobi, Master Yoda, or Anakin Skywalker. He'd searched the HoloNet before and had only come up empty. However, this time he found something. . . .

CHAPTER ELEVEN

Anakin Skywalker — Winner. Time: 15.42:655.

Luke could hardly believe his eyes. His father's name and the words beside it were represented in Aurebesh lettering, suspended in the air above the computer console's holocomm. He'd found the data in an article that had recently been posted by a journalist and former Podracer pilot named Clegg Holdfast. Although Podracing remained illegal throughout the galaxy, the destruction of the second Death Star had apparently emboldened Holdfast to write about the outlawed sport.

Holdfast's article was a history of the Boonta Eve Classic, a once-famous Podrace competition that had been held annually at the Mos Espa Arena on Tatooine for many years. The article provided a list of Boonta winners and other participants. According to the data, Anakin Skywalker's victory had occurred thirty-six years earlier.

Luke studied the article with amazement. After the conflicting accounts he'd heard from his uncle and aunt as well as Ben Kenobi, he'd begun to wonder whether his father had ever been on Tatooine at all. Now it appeared he had proof.

He navigated through the article and found a holographic image and schematics of Anakin Skywalker's Podracer, an open-cockpit repulsorlift chariot reined to two long engines. Unfortunately, Holdfast had not provided any images of Anakin. Examining the schematics for Anakin's chariot, Luke thought, *That can't be right. A person couldn't fit in that contraption.*

And then it hit him. Although the chariot was too small for an adult human, it could fit a child. He recalled what Ben's spirit had told him on Dagobah, just before Luke left to confront Darth Vader at Endor. Ben had said that Anakin was already a great pilot when they'd first met. Luke had assumed he'd meant an adult starpilot.

Could Ben have meant . . . my father was a Podracer pilot?

From personal experience, Luke knew that Podracing was an incredibly dangerous sport. Shortly after the destruction of the first Death Star, circumstances had led him to climb into the cramped cockpit of a Podracer — it had previously belonged to a Dug — and compete in a Podrace on the planet Muunilinst. Even with Jedi reflexes and the Force as his ally, it had taken great effort for Luke to survive that day. Although he could imagine young Anakin fitting into a Podracer's cockpit, he couldn't think of any good reason why a child would have been allowed behind the controls.

Luke scanned through the data in Holdfast's article. According to Holdfast, the Mos Espa Arena had become a track for swoop bike races, and two veteran pilots of the Boonta were currently employed as mechanics.

Luke decided right then that he was overdue for a vacation.

"Master Luke!" C-3PO said as he entered the hangar in the *New Hope*. "I've been looking for you all over the ship."

"Looks like you found me."

Luke was standing beside a ladder that extended up to the cockpit of his X-wing starfighter. While a team of technicians lowered R2-D2 into the socket behind the X-wing's cockpit, C-3PO said, "Sir, it appears you are . . . going somewhere?"

"Very perceptive, Threepio."

Planted in his socket, R2-D2 rotated his domed head and emitted a digital chirp.

"What?" C-3PO said with surprise. "You're going to Tatooine?"

"That's right," Luke said. "There's something I need to investigate there."

"But, sir, I just received word from Princess Leia. She has requested your presence on Aridus."

"Why?"

"A meeting with the Chubbits. There are several Chubbits who remember you well from your previous visit. The princess thinks your presence might —"

"Tell her I'm unavailable," Luke said, pulling on his helmet.

"But, sir, I had the distinct impression that the princess hoped you would —"

"Just *tell* her, Threepio," Luke said as he climbed up to the cockpit. "If anything really urgent comes up, she can contact me on the emergency frequency."

"Emergency frequency?" C-3PO said. "Oh, dear. I can't imagine what her response will be." As Luke was lowering himself behind the X-wing's controls, C-3PO added, "Wait!"

"What is it now?"

"Sir, may I ask the nature of your mission? In case the princess inquires?"

Because Leia had expressed no interest in learning more about the life of Anakin Skywalker, Luke knew that she would probably get upset or angry if she learned why he was going to Tatooine. "It's personal," he said. "But don't worry. I shouldn't be gone more than a couple of days." He lowered the cockpit canopy.

"Don't worry?" C-3PO shook his head. "Oh, dear,

oh, dear." He looked at R2-D2, whose domed head stuck up behind the cockpit. "Artoo-Detoo, you *know* how nervous I get when anyone tells me that. Promise me you'll look after Master Luke."

The astromech replied with a sputtering beep.

"What? Me? An old nanny droid?" As the X-wing lifted off and began moving out of the hangar, C-3PO replied with obvious outrage, "Well, *you* . . . you can go jump in a Sarlacc. See if I care!"

CHAPTER TWELVE

I'm never coming back to this planet again.

Luke shook his head as he recalled the words he'd said to Ben Kenobi more than four years earlier, shortly before they'd blasted out of Mos Eisley Spaceport on the *Millennium Falcon*. Luke had returned several times to Tatooine since that day, and every time, he reminded himself, *Never say never.*

R2-D2 beeped from his socket. Luke glanced at the translation readout and replied, "Thanks for the offer, but I'll keep the controls on manual." Luke grinned. Sometimes he got the impression that the astromech enjoyed flying the X-wing as much as he did.

He landed his X-wing on the flat roof of the Mos Espa Grand Arena complex, a massive structure located several kilometers from Mos Espa Spaceport, at the junction of the Xelric Draw and the Northern Dune Sea. The complex consisted of several domed buildings and grandstands that overlooked a wide track. The grandstands had been built to accommodate more than 100,000 spectators, but now all the seats were empty.

"Stay with the ship, Artoo," Luke said as he climbed out of the cockpit, taking his dark robe with him. "I'm going to look around."

The astromech droid rattled in his socket behind the cockpit and beeped in protest.

"I didn't ask for your opinion," Luke said as he pulled on his robe and adjusted it to conceal the lightsaber at his belt. "I'm telling you to stay here. If any vandals come poking around the ship, you have my permission to zap 'em. All right?"

R2-D2 stopped rattling and responded with another series of beeps. To Luke's ears, it sounded as if the droid was actually happy about the possibility of using his retractable power-charge arm against thieves.

Luke walked alongside the roof's railed edge as he headed for a large domed structure that jutted up above roof level. He gazed out over the empty grandstands and studied the arena's wide, dilapidated speedway. To his right, the track curved off and vanished amid rocky pinnacles, and to his left, it curved back toward the immense plain known as Hutt Flats.

He heard a noise across the distance, the distinctive whine of swoop bikes, which were essentially long, powerful engines with seats on their backs. A moment later, he saw two swoop bikes zoom in from the Flats, carrying their riders past the grandstands before they sped under the broad expanse of an elevated footbridge that served as the finish line.

As the swoops came to a stop, Luke heard a woman's voice nearby. "Looking for something, mister?"

Luke turned to see a tall, slender woman standing outside a doorway to the domed building. She wore a strangely elegant jacket and dress, and from the way she held one hand behind her back, Luke assumed she was holding a weapon. "Hello," he said. "Yes, I'm hoping to find Ody Mandrell and Teemto Pagalies."

The woman looked at Luke suspiciously. "Who are you, and what do you want with them?"

Because Luke was an enemy of the Empire and cautious, he wasn't about to reveal his real name. "My name is Lars," he said. "A journalist named Clegg Holdfast wrote about this place, and I just wanted to talk with some of the old Podracer pilots."

"Really?" the woman said. Looking past Luke, she asked, "Is that your droid and starfighter parked on my roof over there?"

Luke glanced over his shoulder and saw R2-D2 beside the X-wing. Then he looked back at the woman, who had moved her body slightly so he now saw the grip of a compact blaster pistol in her hand. He couldn't blame her for being suspicious of strangers, but he also wanted to avoid a violent confrontation. He said, "May I ask your name?"

"Ulda," she said. "And you're trespassing on my property."

"You *own* all this?"

"Keep your hands where I can see them," Ulda said as she shifted her arm to level her pistol at Luke.

"Well, Ulda," Luke said as raised his hands and looked straight into the woman's eyes, "I don't see a starfighter or a droid on the roof."

Ulda looked past Luke again, then repeated, "I don't see a starfighter or a droid on the roof."

"I'm not going to harm you."

"I'm not going to harm you," the woman repeated as she placed the pistol into a jacket pocket.

"You can direct me to Ody Mandrell and Teemto Pagalies."

"Yes, I can direct you to them," Ulda said pleasantly. She was completely unaware that Luke was using the Force to gently manipulate her mind. She walked to the rail beside Luke and pointed down to the two swoop bikes that rested beyond the finish line. "There they are."

"Do we remember Anakin Skywalker?" Teemto Pagalies said. Standing beside his swoop bike on the speedway in the shadow of the arena's grandstand, he glanced at Ody Mandrell. "Ha! How could we forget him?"

150

Ody rolled his eyes as he aimed a thumb at Teemto and said to Luke, "I remember more than *this* guy about the race that Skywalker won."

Ody Mandrell, who stood slightly shorter than Luke, was an Er'Kit, a species characterized by pale gray skin and downward-pointed ears. Teemto was a Veknoid who was shorter than Ody and had a head that was mostly jaw. Teemto had also lost an eye, an arm, and both ears, and bore numerous scars — all mementos of his Podracing days.

Ody threw a friendly chuck at Teemto's shoulder and said, "Go on, tell us how well you remember *anything* after the Sand People blasted you at Canyon Dune Turn."

"But I also raced Skywalker *before* the Boonta!" Teemto said. "And I *didn't* forget that! Oh, and about the Boonta? I also remember *you* were disqualified because some pit droid got sucked into one of your engine intakes!"

"Sure, you remember," Ody laughed. "But only because I told you."

Teemto looked at Luke and said, "What do you wanna know about Skywalker?"

"Well," Luke said, "do you know how old he was when he won the race?"

The veteran Podracers answered at the same time. Ody said, "Nine." Teemto said, "Ten."

Luke smiled. "What was he like?"

Without hesitation, Teemto said, "A total demon."

"Demon?"

"Yeah, you know . . . a speed demon," Ody said. "It's a compliment."

Teemto said, "And that little human, he never cheated in a race."

"Ever!" Ody added. "Even when he had the chance! Most of us just did whatever we could to make it over the finish line. Say, did you ever see a Podrace?"

Luke thought of his own experience in a Podracer on Muunilinst and tried not to grin. He said, "I've seen a few, but . . . nothing like what you guys must have done. From what I've heard, I'm afraid most of the greatest Podraces happened before I was born."

Ody shook his head sadly. "Ain't that the lousy truth, brother."

"Hey!" Teemto said. "I just remembered: I have a vidrecording of the Boonta in the garage. You want a copy? Some great views of Skywalker's Podracer."

"Yes, please," Luke said. "I'd appreciate that very much."

"Be right back."

While Teemto hobbled off, Luke faced Ody and said, "Do you know if Anakin lived on Tatooine?"

Ody nodded. "Sure, right in Mos Espa Spaceport. I saw him a few times at Watto's junk shop. I got parts for my Podracer engine there." Ody scratched his head. "I

152

think his mother worked at Watto's too. Gosh, that was a long time ago."

"Anakin's mother?" Luke said. "Was her name Shmi?"

Ody shook his head. "I can't recall. Like I said . . . a lot of years have passed. But if you want to find out more, you should go to Watto's and . . ." Ody clapped his hand against his forehead. "Sorry, I keep forgetting. It's not Watto's anymore. It's Wald's."

"Wald's?"

"Yeah, Watto retired. Now it's Wald's Parts. But that's why you should go there. Wald knew Anakin. Let me give you directions. . . ."

Just as Ody finished telling Luke where to find the junk dealership, Teemto came walking back with a datatape. Handing it to Luke, he said, "Here ya go. A Boonta classic."

"Thank you," Luke said. "I'd like to pay you for this."

Teemto held up his one hand and said, "Keep your credits. Just tell all your friends to visit Mos Espa Arena for the swoop races."

"I'll do that," Luke said. "Thanks again." He bowed his head politely, then turned and walked off to return to his X-wing, eager to meet with Wald.

CHAPTER THIRTEEN

As Luke's X-wing carried him and R2-D2 away from the roof of the grand arena, Luke said, "Artoo, we're going to Mos Espa Spaceport. I need to visit a junk dealer in the southwest district."

R2-D2 responded with an inquisitive beep via the comm. Luke glanced at a rectangular monitor on the starfighter's control console to see small red letterforms appear, an Aurebesh translation of the droid's question.

Luke replied, "The junk dealer's name is Wald."

R2-D2 beeped again, and Luke read another question.

"Actually, someone named Watto used to own the place. Why are you so interested?"

The droid beeped yet again.

"But if you go with me, you'll just get sand in your joints."

R2-D2 protested so furiously that Luke didn't need to read the translation.

"All right, enough already!" Luke said. "Have it your way." Sometimes R2-D2 just baffled him.

Mos Espa Spaceport was a wide sprawl of mostly domed buildings made of pourstone. Luke landed the X-wing in an empty docking bay and helped R2-D2 out of the socket and down to the ground. They exited the docking bay and proceed to their next destination.

Numerous human, alien, and droid pedestrians moved about the dusty streets of Mos Espa, and no one paid any notice to the robed stranger or his droid companion. Following the directions Ody Mandrell had given him, Luke found the junk shop without difficulty.

Wald's Parts was a bell-shaped domed building that was connected to an outdoor junkyard. R2-D2 followed Luke through the building's entrance portal, and they arrived in a chamber that was completely cluttered by metal scrap and odd bits of machinery from many different worlds. It reminded Luke of the tech dome on the Lars homestead, only much better stocked and far less organized. He thought, *When I was little, I would have loved this place!*

Luke heard footsteps and turned to see a Rodian enter the chamber from a back room. A green-skinned humanoid with large multifaceted eyes and a flexible snout, the Rodian saw Luke and said, "Help you?"

"Yes," Luke said. "My name is Lars. Are you Wald?"

"I am," the Rodian said. "Just like the sign says." He gestured to a sculptural sign that hung on the wall.

Luke hadn't noticed the sign because of all the scrap that surrounded it. The sign was composed of bent-metal Aurebesh letters that spelled out *Wald's Parts*, but Luke could tell from the rudimentary craftsmanship that some of the letters had been recycled from the shop's previous name.

Wald noticed the astromech droid beside Luke and said, "If you're interested in selling that droid, you came to the right place."

R2-D2 let out a panicked whistle and began beeping furiously.

"Calm down," Luke said to R2-D2. "*You're* the one who wanted to tag along." Looking at Wald, Luke said, "No, the droid's not for sale."

"Then how can I help you?"

"I'm trying to find out some information about a Podracer pilot named Anakin Skywalker. I just came from the Mos Espa Arena. Ody Mandrell and Teemto Pagalies, they told me that Anakin's mother used to work here, and that you knew him."

The Rodian snorted. "Ody and Teemto talk too much," he said. "But yeah, it's true. I knew Anakin. I was only six years old when he left Tatooine. Did Ody and Teemto tell you that I helped build Anakin's Podracer?"

"No, they didn't. When exactly did Anakin leave?"

156

"The same day he won," Wald said. The corners of his snout flexed into something that resembled a smile. "When he crossed that finish line, that may have been just about the proudest moment of my life."

"You were proud because you helped him build the winning Podracer?"

"He didn't just win the Boonta," Wald said. "He won his freedom."

"Oh?" Luke said. "In what way?"

"Watto, the Toydarian who used to own this place, he owned Anakin too."

"Sorry," Luke said. "Did you say *owned*?"

Wald nodded. "Anakin was Watto's slave."

Luke was stunned. He said, "Then . . . Anakin's mother? Shmi? She was a slave too?"

"That's right," Wald said. "And from the look on your face, I guess you didn't know that either."

Luke shook his head.

"You shouldn't be so stunned. There are lots of former slaves in Mos Espa, myself included."

Luke was silent for a moment, then he said, "I'm sorry. I had no idea."

Wald chuckled. "Nothing for you to be sorry about. It wasn't your fault. Anyway, things turned out pretty well for Anakin. He won his freedom and left the same day."

"Left?" Luke said. "With his mother?"

"No," Wald said. "You probably won't believe this,

157

but he left with a Jedi. At least that's what another friend of ours, Kitster, told me. Ah, but a fellow as young as yourself, I doubt you even know about Jedi."

Luke almost smiled at this. He said, "Actually, I have heard of them. Do you recall the Jedi's name? The one who left with Anakin?"

"Can't say I do," Wald said. "He was a big human, broad face, had a beard."

"Big? Do you mean he was tall?"

Wald chuckled again. "I was six years old at the time. Most adults looked like giants. But I remember seeing him step out of Anakin's place, and this Jedi guy, he had to duck his head through the doorway. I thought, 'That's a big human.' "

Luke doubted that the Jedi had been Obi-Wan. He said, "So, did Anakin win his mother's freedom too?"

"No, she was still a slave, but not for long."

"The Jedi helped her?"

"Yeah," Wald said. "Someone — probably Kitster, the friend I mentioned — told me that the Jedi sent a gift to Shmi, something she could use to buy her freedom. But she stayed with Watto for a few more years."

Baffled, Luke said, "Why?"

Wald shrugged. "Maybe she had nowhere else to go. Also, Watto wasn't all that bad." Then Wald smiled. "She was a terrific lady. She gave me some of Anakin's tools. If it weren't for her, I might not have wound up working here and gaining my own freedom. But to make a long story short, she finally gained *her* freedom, and married Cliegg Lars, a moisture farmer. I went to their wedding in Anchorhead." Wald narrowed his gaze on Luke's features. "Say, didn't you say your name was Lars? Maybe you're related?"

"What?" Luke said. His memory flashed to the unmarked graves on the Lars homestead, and he wished he'd chosen a different name when he'd introduced himself to the Rodian. "Yes . . . but no. I mean, I'm Lars, but no relation. At least . . . I don't think so."

"Yeah, well, I don't see any resemblance." Wald shook his head sadly and said, "It was awful, how Shmi died."

Luke didn't want to ask, but he had to know. "How?"

"Sand People abducted her from the Lars farm," Wald said. "Took her off into the desert and killed her."

The Rodian's words jolted Luke. He could only imagine where Shmi's death might have occurred, but he suddenly recalled the remote, abandoned Tusken Raider camp that he and Biggs had discovered in the Jundland Wastes years earlier. His legs felt weak. He placed one hand on top of R2-D2's domed head to steady himself.

"I have to go," Luke said. "Thank you . . . for your time."

Wald said, "You all right?"

"Air," Luke said absently. "I need some." He turned and staggered out of the shop. R2-D2 followed.

The air outside was even hotter than in the shop, but Luke took a deep breath anyway. He had spent so many years wondering about the life of Anakin Skywalker and had been so excited when he'd discovered that his father had been a Podracer pilot on Tatooine. Now he just felt drained and exhausted.

My father and his mother were slaves. How awful for them.

And then he felt outraged. Not just because of the injustice of Anakin and Shmi's circumstances, but because Owen and Beru had never told him. But then he wondered, *Did they even know that Shmi had been a slave before she married Owen's father? Did Ben have any idea? He must have!* He glanced back at the junk shop, thought of more questions that he might have asked Wald, and then shook his head and looked away.

He realized he wasn't angry with Owen, Beru, or Ben for that matter. He knew in his heart that there was a reason they had not told him the truth about so many things. They'd only been doing what they'd thought was best to protect him.

He reflected on how Owen used to get anxious to the point of fury when Luke strayed from home. *If I'd known how my grandmother died, I might have been more considerate.*

R2-D2 rotated his dome to gaze at Luke through his photoreceptor. The droid emitted a somber-sounding, muffled beep.

Luke said, "C'mon, Artoo."

They returned to the docking bay. After Luke got R2-D2 back into the X-wing's astromech socket, he climbed into the starfighter's cockpit and saw a red light flashing on his comm. Someone was trying to contact him on the emergency frequency.

He pressed a button. A moment later, a man's familiar voice crackled from the comm. "Luke? Do you read me?"

"I read you, Han," Luke said, "but just barely. There's a lot of atmospheric interference." He was glad to be talking with his friend Han Solo, but given that they were communicating via the emergency frequency, he was also concerned about what Han might have to say.

"Goldenrod told —" Han's words were interrupted by a burst of static before his voice continued, "— on Tatooine."

Luke knew that "Goldenrod" was Han's nickname for C-3PO. Speaking to the droid behind him, Luke said, "Artoo, try to boost the signal."

R2-D2 beeped agreeably and extended an antenna from his dome.

Luke said, "Han, I'm still on Tatooine. What's wrong?"

Sounding slightly clearer, Han answered, "A possible situation on Tarnoonga."

"What happened?" Luke said. He knew that Tarnoonga was a water world in the Arkanis Sector, the same sector that contained the Tatooine system.

There was another burst of static; then Han's voice returned. "— lost contact with two Alliance scouts. In the last report from Tarnoonga, one of the scouts said they'd found what looked like an abandoned Imperial outpost before they were attacked by an Oskan blood eater."

Luke had never encountered any Oskan blood eaters, but knew from holovids that they were monstrous four-armed beasts with a taste for humans. Because the earliest recorded sighting of a blood eater was barely twenty-five years old, and because the creatures had since been discovered on the grounds of Imperial penal colonies on numerous worlds, it was rumored that they were artificially created life-forms developed by the Empire.

Luke said, "Were the scouts injured?"

"Incredibly, no," Han said, but quickly added, "At least we don't think so. According to the report, an unidentified woman killed the creature before it could harm anyone."

"Well, that's a relief," Luke said. "Sounds like we may have found a new ally."

"Let's hope so," Han said. "Before we lost contact, the scout said the woman use —"

More static.

"What?" Luke said. "What did the scout say about the woman?"

"A lightsaber, Luke!" Han said. "The woman used a lightsa —"

There was a loud static burst, and then the transmission went dead.

CHAPTER FOURTEEN

"Han? Han!" Still seated in his X-wing's cockpit in the Mos Espa docking bay, Luke groaned in frustration with the broken connection.

In the socket behind the cockpit, R2-D2 beeped.

Luke looked at the rectangular monitor on his console to read the droid's question, then replied, "Yes, it could be a trap, Artoo. But then again, there could also be two scouts who need our help." As he lowered the cockpit canopy, he added, "I don't have coordinates for Tarnoonga's star system, but I know all the stars in the Arkanis Sector by sight. I'll be able to spot it after we reach space, and you can plot a course from there."

R2-D2 beeped again.

Luke read the droid's response, then said, "What do you mean, you know the way to Tarnoonga? You've been there before?"

The astromech gave an affirmative whistle.

Luke grinned. "One of these days, you'll have to tell me about your exploits before we met." He started the X-wing's engines. The starfighter lifted out of the docking bay, then ascended from the spaceport into space.

Because he had only recently left a desert planet, Luke felt jolted by the sight of the ocean-covered Tarnoonga, which appeared to be in every way Tatooine's opposite. Gray skies hung over the dark, watery surface, and a lightning storm loomed on the horizon. The only visible land masses were the uppermost areas of otherwise submerged mountain ranges.

As the X-wing cut through the windy turbulence high over the roiling seas, Luke said, "Artoo, any luck contacting Han?"

The droid replied with a negative whistle.

Luke grimaced. He had hoped to reestablish communication with Han Solo after leaving Tatooine, but the only thing that came over the emergency frequency was static. Now the atmospheric conditions on Tarnoonga seemed to prohibit a clear transmission too.

A light pulsed on Luke's comm console. "It's a signal from an Alliance distress beacon, Artoo! At least we're receiving some kind of transmission clearly. Can you home in on it?"

The droid beeped, and then Luke saw a map appear on his console. On the map, a blue blip winked on and off to the east of the X-wing's position.

Luke turned his head to gaze out the cockpit's view-port and saw what appeared to be an island of jagged rock formations. It was the top of a mountain range that was approximately three kilometers long and almost half as wide. High black cliffs plummeted to the dark water below.

"It's coming from that range," Luke said. "Maybe the scouts landed their ship there. Let's see if we can spot it."

They flew over the mountain range's craggy terrain. It didn't take them long to find the ship. It was an old Corellian G9 Rigger freighter, resting on a wide black slab of rock that appeared to be partially protected from the winds by a natural outcropping. Luke couldn't see anything that looked like an abandoned Imperial out-post, which Han had mentioned when he'd relayed the missing scouts' report, or any other architectural struc-tures. Luke allowed the possibility that the alleged outpost was camouflaged or underground.

R2-D2 helped guide the X-wing down beside the other ship. Although the freighter's hull had seen better days, it didn't appear to be damaged. Luke noticed that its landing ramp was down.

Still seated in the X-wing's cockpit, Luke checked his scopes. "No life signs on their ship, Artoo. And the beacon's signal is coming from somewhere else. You stay put while I check out the ship and look for the beacon. It can't be far. If I find anyone or see any blood eaters, I'll let you know."

As Luke unlocked the cockpit canopy, R2-D2 responded with a spurt of excited beeps.

Luke consulted the monitor to read the translation of the droid's message, then said, "No, I definitely *haven't* forgotten what Han said about a woman with a lightsaber."

The astromech emitted more excited beeps.

"No more arguments!" Luke said. "Your job is to stay here and keep trying to contact Han. I'll check in with you every fifteen minutes. If you don't hear back from me, take the X-wing into orbit and let the Alliance know where I am. Got that?"

The droid emitted a whimpering whistle.

"All right, then," Luke said. He checked his light-saber and comlink, then climbed out of the cockpit, taking his robe with him. As he stepped down to the black rock, he noticed that his legs ached a bit because he'd been traveling in such a cramped cockpit. It was chilly outside. He pulled on his robe quickly, then walked cautiously toward the freighter.

Luke drew his lightsaber as he stepped up the freighter's landing ramp. He moved cautiously through the ship, searching for any sign of the scouts. Upon entering the bridge, he was alarmed to see the scorched remains of the controls and communication consoles. It looked like someone had fired a blaster at almost point-blank range into the instruments.

Luke had never heard of blood eaters using blasters. He wondered, *Did the scouts do this? Or someone else?*

Exiting the freighter, he resecured his lightsaber to his belt. He walked away from the two ships, moving around the outcropping until he reached a gulley that led him up over the mountain's southern shoulder. Although fifteen minutes had yet to pass, he activated his comlink and said, "Do you read me, Artoo?"

R2-D2 beeped in response.

"I'm fine," Luke said. "Just testing the comlink." He returned the comlink to his belt before he moved on, heading for a notch between two stony ridges.

He kept his eyes peeled for anything unusual. The landscape was littered with broken black stones. Except for a few small patches of moss, there wasn't any sign of life. Luke wondered why Imperial soldiers might have brought an Oskan blood eater to Tarnoonga.

The clouds overhead became darker. Luke thought again about the report Han had relayed to him. *Could the scouts have really seen a Jedi? Or was it something else?* He realized that his heart was pounding unusually fast. He didn't stop walking but took a deep breath to calm himself.

He spied a small glint of silvery metal against the bleak terrain. He soon arrived at the thing that had caused the glint. It was a little box-shaped object, which rested on the ground between two stones. The object was slightly smaller than his comlink, and he recognized it as a compact emergency beacon.

He picked up the beacon and examined it. It didn't appear to be damaged. Because the transmitter would have been more effective if it had been placed in a more elevated position, he wondered if one of the scouts had accidentally dropped the device. *Maybe they didn't have time to think about where to put it.* He turned in place, scanning the surrounding area for any sign of movement. He saw none. He considered switching off the beacon but decided to leave it activated before he placed it in one of his robe's pockets.

And then he heard an inhuman roar behind him.

Luke turned fast to see the blood eater running at him. The hulking beast was well over two and a half meters tall. Each of its four arms was tapered into a bladelike claw. Its hunched shoulders were topped by a gaping mouth with concentric layers of razor-sharp teeth instead of a head.

Luke did not pause to wonder where the creature had come from or how it had snuck up on him so fast without making a sound. His hand simply flashed to his lightsaber and he ignited its blade.

The blood eater's upper left and lower right arms lashed out at Luke. Luke ducked to avoid one arm as he brought his lightsaber up fast to deflect the other. The blood eater howled as Luke's blade cleaved through a thick layer of skin. Then it swung its other claw-tipped arms at Luke.

Luke jumped and rolled aside as the monster's claws smashed down into the ground. He sprang to his feet, bracing himself for another onslaught, but then he heard a sound behind him, the distinctive burst and hum of a just-activated lightsaber.

The blood eater stopped dead in its tracks. Luke froze.

And then Luke saw a blue-robed woman leap past him. A hood obscured her face, but, because she was wielding a lightsaber, Luke believed that she had to be the woman who reportedly had rescued the Alliance scouts.

Luke angled his own lightsaber away as the hooded woman swung her lightsaber at the blood eater. The blue energy blade swept through one clawed arm at the elbow. The blood eater yowled as its severed arm fell to the ground, and, at the same time, it reflexively swung one of its other claws out at its attacker.

Luke gasped as the blood eater's blow connected, sending the blue-robed woman flying into a wall of rock. The woman's lightsaber spiraled away through the air and automatically deactivated as the woman collapsed upon the rocky ground.

The blood eater howled with rage. Luke jumped forward, raising his lightsaber so that its tip was aimed straight at the monster's broad chest. The blood eater snatched up its severed claw as it backed away from Luke, then turned quickly and scurried away over the rocks.

Luke looked from the fleeing monster to the woman, who was now sprawled on the ground, lying face-down. She didn't move. Luke glanced back to where he had last seen the blood eater. The wounded monster had vanished. Then Luke looked at the area where he'd seen the woman's lightsaber fall, and he saw that it was gone too.

But where? Did the blood eater take it?

Luke deactivated his lightsaber and crouched down beside the motionless woman's prone form. He gently rolled her body over and discovered she was wearing the uniform of an Alliance scout, which Luke found puzzling.

The woman's face was still covered by her hood. She moaned. As Luke reached up to push her hood back, he said, "Are you all right?"

And then he saw her face. He recognized her immediately, even before she opened the ice blue eyes that he had not seen since he'd buried her on Hoth.

She was Frija.

CHAPTER FIFTEEN

Luke was stunned. "Frija?"

The woman's eyes opened wide with surprise. "You . . . you're Luke Skywalker."

Her voice was just as he'd remembered it. He tore his gaze from her to scan the area again, searching and listening for the blood eater. He saw only masses of dark rock and the shadows between them. The creature seemed to be as stealthy as it was deadly.

Luke returned his attention to Frija and helped her up from the ground. He said, "How . . . how did you survive? And where did you get the lightsaber?"

"The lightsaber!" Frija said. Her hands flashed out to her sides. "Where is it? Oh, no, I lost it!"

"I think the blood eater got it," Luke said. "But hang on, how did you survive after —"

"The lightsaber," Frija interrupted, "it belonged to the Jedi who saved me and Levlonn, the scout who was with me. But another blood eater killed the Jedi and . . .

it got Levlonn too. I only used the lightsaber because my blaster's power cell died."

The information was more than Luke could comprehend. "Wait. Let's start with how you're still alive. When I left you on —"

"We can't stay here!" Frija said frantically. "There are at least five blood eaters in the area. They *will* come back. Where's your ship?"

"I landed next to yours," Luke said. "But mine's an X-wing. I'm afraid it won't hold both of —"

They heard a shuffling sound behind some nearby rocks. Frija grabbed Luke's wrist, tugged it sharply, and said, "Hurry!"

A low growl sounded from behind, and they ran in the opposite direction, heading away from the landing site. Luke sprinted alongside Frija as she held tight to his wrist, guiding him around a series of mammoth boulders.

Luke said, "Where're we going?"

"Someplace safe."

"We should go back to the ships!"

"We'd never make it!"

"How did the blood eaters get —"

"Stop talking! Just run!"

They didn't stop running until they arrived at a high wall of stone that was topped by a wide overhang. At the wall's base was a black slit, a crevice less than a meter wide.

"Inside!" Frija said breathlessly, tugging Luke after her as she moved into the narrow passage.

The crevice turned out to be the entrance to a cave. They arrived in a large smooth-walled chamber that was without windows and illuminated by a single glowlamp. The glowlamp was propped up against a wall beside several cargo containers. All the containers bore an Imperial insignia. A stairwell was carved into one wall, and the stone steps descended into darkness.

"This is the abandoned outpost?"

Frija nodded. "The blood eaters can't follow us in here. Are you all right?"

"Yes, but . . . I still don't understand." Luke looked at Frija cautiously. "How did you get here from Hoth?"

"Hoth?" Now it was Frija who looked confused. "What are you talking about?"

"But, Frija, I —"

"And how do you know my name?" Frija interrupted. "We've never met before."

Even more baffled, Luke said, "But I thought . . . you recognized me. After the blood eater fled, and I helped you up, you said my name."

"Yes, but you're . . . well, you're *Luke Skywalker,*" Frija said. "Everyone in the Alliance knows what you look like. I've seen you on vidrecordings."

"Vidrecordings?" Luke's brow furrowed as he tried to make sense of it all. He suddenly realized that there was only one reasonable explanation for the woman who stood before him. "Your father. He was an Imperial governor?"

Frija looked at Luke warily, then said, "Yes, but that's no secret. The Alliance is aware of who my father was."

"Please, give me a moment." Luke took a deep breath as he tried to collect his thoughts. "Your human replica droid. I met her. On Hoth, an ice planet in the Anoat Sector. She was with the replica of your father. She told me how the Empire had created them as decoys. You look like . . . I mean, the *droid* looked just like you."

"Oh, my," Frija said. "Is she . . . are the droids still . . . active?"

Luke shook his head. "They're both gone. I buried them on Hoth."

Frija sighed. "To my father, they were just part of his own elaborate escape plan," she said sadly. "But I could never think of them as mere machines. They were too . . . too real. Especially my own counterpart. If any droid ever possessed genuine feelings, it was her."

Luke had thought the same thing. He said, "What happened to your father?"

"He made the mistake of betraying the Emperor. He tried to deliver some secret plans to the Rebel Alliance. The Emperor had him killed."

"I'm sorry."

"I joined the Alliance right after that. I knew it was the right thing to do. I wanted to make a difference."

Luke had previously wondered what had become of the droid Frija's human counterpart, whether she and her father had successfully escaped from the Rebels or the Imperials, or whatever they'd been running from. He had even consulted Alliance Intelligence to find out if they had any information about a renegade Imperial governor and his daughter. They hadn't been able to turn up anything useful. And yet here she was before him, just as kind and brave as the Frija he'd known on Hoth.

But he still had questions for her. "The lightsaber you used," he said. "Can you describe the person you took it from?"

Frija nodded. "A woman who wore a black cloak. I only glimpsed her face. She had fair skin. She appeared from out of nowhere, just a moment after the first blood eater attacked me and Levlonn." Frija bit her lower lip nervously.

"This woman," Luke said. "She actually identified herself as a Jedi?"

"She had a lightsaber. What else could she have been?"

"I don't know," Luke said, but he hoped she hadn't been a Sith disciple like Lumiya. "Go on."

"She told us to run for cover. Levlonn and I ran for

our ship. I glanced back and saw the Jedi kill the blood eater. We immediately transmitted a report back to the *New Hope*. Is that how you found out about us?"

Luke nodded.

"We were still transmitting," Frija continued, "when we heard a scream from outside our ship. It was her. The Jedi. We searched for her body, but all we found was her weapon. I picked it up and . . ." Frija's eyes widened.

"What happened?"

"And then . . . and then they came. The other blood eaters . . . they came at us! We got back onto our ship, but two of them got inside. We exhausted our blasters on them. We . . . I . . ." Her entire body began to tremble. "I got away. Levlonn didn't."

Luke stepped closer to Frija. "I'm sorry about your partner," he said as he placed his hands on her shoulders. "You're safe now."

"Oh, Luke." She reached her arms around him and held him tight. "I'm so frightened."

The glowlamp was behind Frija, and, as Luke looked into its light, he suddenly had a feeling that he was overlooking some crucial detail. It wasn't that he doubted Frija, but he thought something was missing in her account of the lightsaber-wielding defender. Granted, he'd seen the lightsaber, but that was hardly evidence that the mysterious woman had been a Jedi.

He pulled back slightly, holding Frija at arm's length. "Listen," he said, "this might be important. You didn't actually see the blood eaters kill the Jedi?"

"No, I didn't."

"Do you think it's possible she's still alive?" Before Frija could answer, Luke's comlink emitted an electronic chirp. "Oh, no," Luke said. "I forgot all about Artoo!" He took his comlink from his belt and spoke into it. "Artoo, do you read me? Artoo?" Hearing no response, he shook the device, then repeated, "Do you read me?"

If R2-D2 gave an answer, Luke didn't hear it. Instead, he heard a loud roar echo down through the passage that had delivered them to the underground chamber.

"The blood eaters!" Frija said with alarm.

And then they heard a loud slam, like a massive hammer striking the chamber's outer wall. The noise was followed by another slam, and then another. Looking toward the passage, Luke returned the comlink to his belt as he said, "That sounds more like a krayt dragon."

"A what?"

"A creature from Tatooine," he said. "Whatever it is, it's big."

The pounding noise continued and intensified. Frija said, "It's going to break through!" She turned and ran for the stairwell and plunged down the stone steps.

"Wait!" Luke said as Frija vanished into the darkness. He bent fast to pick up the glowlamp, but, as he angled its light into the stairwell and was about to follow Frija, he caught himself.

He tightened his grip on the glowlamp. He realized he had found the overlooked detail.

The hammering was now an almost deafening din. Luke ignored it and stepped over to one of the Imperial cargo containers. With his free hand, he threw back the container's lid. He swept the glowlamp over the container.

It was filled with stormtrooper armor.

He lifted the lid of another container. More white armor. And bones too. Human bones.

Luke released the lid. Suddenly, the thunderous pounding ended. Luke's ears were still ringing as he removed the comlink from his belt. Keeping his voice low, he activated the comlink and said, "Artoo, if you can hear me, leave now. Alert the Alliance to stay away from Tarnoonga. I'll try to find some other way to contact —"

"Luke!" Frija's voice carried up from the open stairwell. "Help me!"

It's a trap, Luke thought as he returned the comlink to his belt. *It was all a trap.*

He stepped away from the cargo containers. He glanced at the crevice that had served as his entrance to the chamber, but he knew he wouldn't get far if he tried to run. There was no way to hide from the thing in the chamber below.

He knew he had to confront it.

Taking the glowlamp with him, Luke followed Frija's path. The stone steps deposited him into a cave that was even darker than the upper room. The air was dank, and he could see pools of stagnant water on the uneven floor. Moving the glowlamp back and forth, he saw a row of ancient architectural columns that rose up to a high ceiling.

Off to his left, something made a dripping noise. Then there came a low growl, and Frija's voice whimpered, "Luke?"

Luke swung the glowlamp to his left and saw a blood eater. It had Frija pinned against one of the columns.

Luke said, "I know that monster isn't real."

"What?" Frija gasped. The blood eater dragged its claws closer against her body and shifted its maw directly over her head. "Luke, please!"

"And I know the Imperial outpost wasn't abandoned," Luke continued. "At least not before you got here."

"It's going to kill me!" Frija cringed as yellow saliva drooled from the blood eater's serrated teeth.

Keeping his voice calm, Luke said, "You made a mistake. You told me you used the lightsaber that you recovered because your blaster's power cell died. Why didn't you transfer the power cell from this glowlamp to your blaster?" He aimed the glowlamp's light directly into Frija's face. "That's what any Alliance scout would have done."

Frija glared at Luke.

"I know what you are," Luke said. "A mind witch."

The glowlamp flickered and went out, and then a wretched cackling echoed through the pitch-black cave. Luke had heard that laugh before.

It was S'ybll's.

CHAPTER SIXTEEN

Luke stood still as the hideous laughter ended. A moment later, the glowlamp flickered back on. The blood eater — or rather the illusion of it — was gone, and Frija had been replaced by S'ybll.

Standing in front of the ancient columns, S'ybll appeared as the same beautiful girl with long dark hair whom Luke recalled from the nameless jungle planet. Evidently, the Alliance scout uniform had also been an illusion, for she was now clad in the animal skins he also remembered.

"Expecting a *different* mind witch, Luke?"

He was stunned. "I saw your corpse . . . buried under a stone. I wasn't the only one. My friends saw you dead too."

S'ybll lifted an eyebrow. "You, Han Solo, and the Wookiee . . . you saw what I wanted you to see. I was injured and severely weakened, that's all. Weak enough that you and your friends *could* have killed me. I had just enough strength to conjure the illusion of my death so I could slip away and lick my wounds. And wait for someone else to find me."

Luke remembered the cargo containers upstairs. "The Imperials," he said. "They must have gone looking for their missing shuttle, the one that you destroyed. But instead of killing the new arrivals . . . you tricked them. Maybe killed just one and then impersonated him so you could leave with the others. They brought you here. And then you killed them all."

"It wasn't a direct flight," S'ybll said, "but your summary of events is remarkably accurate." She smiled. "You'd make an excellent mind witch."

The air suddenly became chilly. Luke said, "What do you want, S'ybll? Revenge? Is that it?"

S'ybll winced as if she found the idea distasteful. "No, not at all." She took a single step away from the columns, and Luke took a cautious step backward. "Actually," she continued, "I was thinking of something more along the lines of . . . an alliance."

"An alliance! You can't mean that we might . . ." Luke's words caught in his throat. In all the excitement, he'd forgotten about —

"Yes," S'ybll said as she read his mind. "The two Alliance scouts. After they arrived, I created an illusion of a female Jedi for them to see. I knew they'd report it, and that the report would lure you here."

Luke scowled. "What have you done with them?"

"See for yourself." She made a sweeping gesture with one hand, and the cave floor beneath Luke's feet began to rumble and shift.

Luke stepped back onto firm ground and watched as a large rectangular section of duracrete flooring slid back into a hidden recess, revealing a deep, steep-walled pit. Shifting the glowlamp to his left hand, he saw two metal-barred cages in the pit. One cage contained two frightened-looking humans, a young woman and a man. He didn't recognize either, but both wore Alliance scout uniforms. The other cage held a blood eater.

Staring down at the pit as if it were nothing more than an architectural curiosity, S'ybll said, "The pit was already here when I arrived. I think these caverns were once a hideout for a gang of pirates."

The male scout turned his head in response to S'ybll's voice and gazed up through the bars of the cage that held him and his fellow scout. "Look!" he said. "It's Luke Skywalker!"

The female scout said, "Thank the stars!"

Luke reached out with the Force. He sensed panic and confusion, and also that the pit and the life-forms in it were not illusions. He returned his gaze to S'ybll.

"Yes, the blood eater is quite real," she said, reading his mind. "The Imperials brought it here. Now it does my bidding."

"Release the scouts, S'ybll."

"As you wish."

From below, the blood eater let out a loud roar. Luke glanced down into the pit and saw that the cage that had held the scouts had vanished, leaving the two scouts standing out in the open. Across from them, the blood eater's claws began hammering at the bars of its own cage.

Directing his gaze to the terrified scouts, Luke said, "Stay calm. Don't move."

S'ybll pouted. "Did I do wrong? You don't want me to let the blood eater know that his cage is just an illusion too, do you?"

Luke moved closer to the edge of the pit, preparing to leap into it and defend the scouts if necessary. Glancing at S'ybll, he said, "Why are you doing this?"

"I told you," she said. "An alliance. Between us."

"For what purpose?"

"You want to defeat the Empire once and for all, don't you? With our combined powers, they wouldn't stand a chance."

Luke looked at her skeptically. "What about what *you* want?"

S'ybll placed her hands on her hips. "It takes a great deal of energy for me to maintain this form and generate illusions. I can't keep living this way, Luke. Waiting for people to find me. That's why I want . . . I *hope* you'll bring them to me."

"You want . . . people?"

"I'd be quite content with undesirable Imperials."

"Somehow I doubt that," Luke said. Shaking his head, he continued, "You're better at casting illusions than telling the truth. If it's people you wanted, you could have tricked the Imperials into flying you to a populated world instead of this one."

S'ybll shrugged. "Just because I need people to survive doesn't mean I like crowds."

Luke thought, *She's insane.*

S'ybll's head snapped back as if she'd been slapped. "Insane? Do you really think so? That's a shame, Luke Skywalker. Because if you don't agree to join me, I . . . well, I just don't know what I might do."

"I'll stand by my thoughts, S'ybll. I won't allow anyone else to fall victim to you."

"So be it."

The blood eater roared again. Luke looked down into the pit to see that the second illusory cage had vanished. Luke did not hesitate. Still clutching the glowlamp in his left hand, he reached for his lightsaber with his right as he sprang forward and leaped down into the pit.

He landed between the blood eater and the two scouts, who fell back against the wall behind him. He cast the glowlamp aside, letting it clatter against the floor, and faced the hulking blood eater as he activated his lightsaber. But as his weapon hummed to life, he was surprised to hear the two scouts shout, "Behind you! Behind you!"

What surprised him was that their excited shouts sounded as if they came from in front of him.

And then the monster attacked.

Luke was knocked off his feet by a massive arm that struck him from behind. He held tight to his lightsaber as his body slammed into the pit's wall and rebounded onto the floor. Recovering his wits as he rolled swiftly to his feet, he realized what had happened. He had been so intent on defending the scouts, he had neglected to consider one of the first lessons Ben Kenobi had taught him about the Force: that his eyes could deceive him. S'ybll had tricked him into mistaking the scouts for the blood eater.

Luke squeezed his eyes closed, calmed his mind, and relaxed his muscles as he reached out with the Force.

He sensed the blood eater coming at him again. But this time, he dodged the claw that had been aimed at his head, and he swung his lightsaber's blade through the monster's arm.

The blood eater howled with pain and rage. Luke heard its wail but kept his eyes shut as he ducked the next incoming claw and swung his blade through one of the monster's legs. The monster howled again as it came crashing down on its wounded appendage. Luke had hoped the monster would surrender, but when he sensed another claw tearing through the air toward his chest, he knew it never would. Not before it tasted blood.

He jumped back to avoid the incoming claw, then kicked off the wall, launching himself over the monster's torso while swinging his lightsaber downward and through the thing's head. Eyes still closed, Luke landed near the two scouts.

The blood eater remained standing on its one leg for a moment, but it was already dead. A moment later, Luke heard the monster's body collapse to the pit floor.

Luke deactivated his lightsaber. Before he could address the scouts, S'ybll called down from above, "You killed my pet. Now I'll have to bury it."

Luke heard a rumbling sound and recognized it as the mechanism for closing the pit's ceiling. But a moment later, he heard an entirely different noise: a loud, explosive rush of water. He was compelled to open his eyes to confirm not only what he sensed through the Force but also what he felt rising up around his boots.

On the opposite wall of the pit, illuminated by the glowlamp that rested nearby, a concealed hatch had opened to release water into the pit. The water pounded against the blood eater's dismembered carcass, sending the body parts, along with the glowlamp, toward Luke and the scouts.

There was a loud slam from above as the pit's ceiling slid closed. Luke turned to face the astonished scouts, still visible by the soft light of the glowlamp. The water level was already up to their waists. As water continued to flood into the pit, the male scout said, "There's no way out!"

"You two stay close to me," Luke said. He kept his lightsaber deactivated but held it above the water with one hand as he used his other to shove one of the blood eater's floating claws aside. "The rising water will carry us up; then I'll cut a hole through the ceiling."

Glancing at Luke's lightsaber, the male scout said, "We're lucky you found us. I'm Andur Thorsim, by the way."

"And I'm Glaennor," said the female scout.

"Glad to know you," Luke said.

Glaennor said, "What's the story with S'ybll? I can't tell if she wants to kiss you or kill you."

"She's a mind witch," Luke said. "Your guess is as good as mine." He kept his lightsaber held high as he and the scouts began treading water. When the gap between the ceiling and the water's surface was just over a meter, he activated his blade and drove it up through the retractable duracrete ceiling. He made a broad circular cut and then pulled his arm back quickly as a thick, disc-shaped piece of duracrete fell into the water, leaving a wide hole overhead.

He deactivated his lightsaber. Casting a quick glance at the scouts, he said, "I'll go up first in case S'ybll's waiting for us, then you follow."

Luke was about to climb up through the hole when Glaennor said, "Something's moving in the water!"

"What?" Luke said. "Where?"

Before Glaennor could answer, a tentacle coiled around Luke's left ankle, and his entire body was yanked below the water's surface. He closed his mouth the moment he went under, but never had the chance to take a deep breath.

The bobbing glowlamp allowed him to see the large tentacled creature that had slipped in through the open hatch. All his senses told him that the creature wasn't an illusion. He didn't recognize the species; he merely knew that he had to free himself from it, and fast, before it yanked him out of the water-filled pit and into some narrow tunnel that lay beyond.

Twisting his body, Luke activated his waterproofed lightsaber and then angled it at the flexible appendage that was coiled around his leg. The lightsaber severed the tentacle, and the creature instantly released Luke before it retracted through the hatch, leaving a thin trail of black blood in its wake.

Luke deactivated his weapon and secured it to his belt as he turned and swam back toward the area where he'd left the scouts. He could see only one figure moving in the murky water, and realized that one scout must have escaped through the hole in the ceiling. He swam down and kicked off the pit's floor, launching himself up with so much force that he nearly hit his head on the duracrete ceiling when he broke the water's surface. The gap had closed to just a few centimeters.

Luke gasped for air as he faced Glaennor, who was still treading water. But then he looked up at the apparently solid ceiling and saw why she had not already exited.

"Andur made it through!" Glaennor said, her eyes wide with fear as she moved beside Luke. "But then the hole sealed itself!"

Luke closed his eyes and reached out with the Force. "It's just an illusion. The hole's over here." Eyes still shut, he reached up with one arm to catch hold of the hole's edges. When he opened his eyes, his arm appeared to be embedded in the ceiling. "C'mon!" he said. "This way! Give me your hand!"

But as he felt Glaennor's hand clamp around his wrist, he saw her suddenly transform into a withered crone with wet, filthy white hair that hung around her leering, skull-like face.

S'ybll!

Luke recoiled and thrashed in the water, trying to free himself from S'ybll's clutches. He knew that she would try to drain him of his life energy if she got her arms around him. But as she held tight and he felt no ill physical effect, he immediately realized that he had allowed his eyes to deceive him again.

He closed his eyes, and the woman swimming beside him shouted, "What's wrong? Why'd you pull away?"

"Sorry, Glaennor!" he said, his eyes still shut as he

reached up through the invisible hole in the ceiling again. "S'ybll made me think you were her."

"Oh," Glaennor said, tilting her head back to lift her chin above the water. "I hope she doesn't do that again."

"Let me handle her. Just hang on!"

Keeping his eyes closed and one hand on Glaennor, Luke hauled himself up through the hole, then pulled her up after him. They were both thoroughly drenched. Luke was doing his best to remain calm when Glaennor screamed, "Andur, look out! Another blood eater!"

And then Luke heard Andur shouting too. Speaking calmly, Luke said, "No. It's just another one of S'ybll's illusions. Just relax and close your eyes."

The two scouts obeyed. A silence fell throughout the cavern. It didn't last long.

"That's right, close your eyes," S'ybll said from a few meters away. Then she cackled and added, "I wouldn't want you to see what's coming."

Luke sensed something large moving fast toward him. It was a block of stone, traveling through the air from near the architectural columns. He threw himself down over Glaennor, shielding her body as the stone sailed over them. A moment later, the stone crashed upon the cavern floor.

Glaennor said, "That didn't sound like an illusion to me!"

"Stay put, and don't move," Luke said as he got up

and stepped aside. He wanted to draw S'ybll's attention away from the scouts.

S'ybll taunted, "Going somewhere, Luke?"

He knew that opening his eyes would be risky, but he did it fast. He saw Andur, who leaned against a nearby wall with his hands held over his eyes, and also S'ybll, who stood before the old columns. Unlike the illusion of the crone he'd seen in the water-filled pit, she still looked young and beautiful.

S'ybll smiled and said, "Our reunion doesn't have to end in death and destruction. My offer of an alliance still stands."

"You never give up, do you?" Luke said. "If you can read my mind, you know that nothing could convince me to join you."

S'ybll arched one eyebrow. "Nothing?"

A light shimmered in the air near Luke, and then a ghostly apparition materialized. It was a man wearing the robes of a Jedi. Luke recognized him. It was his father, Anakin Skywalker.

"Luke," Anakin said. "I know you still have many questions about me."

Luke swallowed hard. He knew that the apparition wasn't really his father's spirit, but . . . *His voice is just as I remembered.*

"I've missed you, son."

Luke tore his eyes from the apparition to face S'ybll.

The apparition said, "Just as you found goodness in me, can you not find any in S'ybll?"

Luke kept his gaze fixed on S'ybll. "No," he said. "I can't. I sense only darkness in you."

S'ybll took a step back, moving closer to the columns.

Watching her, Luke wondered why she was staying so close to the ancient structure. *Does it make her feel protected?* And then the realization hit him. *It gives her power!*

Reading Luke's mind, S'ybll winced. She said, "You're wrong."

The illusion of Anakin Skywalker's spirit vanished.

Luke said, "These columns are identical to the ones at the ruins on the jungle world. What do they do exactly? Increase your psychic abilities?"

"My powers are my own!"

"You came here after you destroyed your old home because you needed a new one, and you knew about *this* place. Now you're afraid of losing power. You're afraid of leaving Tarnoonga."

"I'm afraid of nothing!" S'ybll extended her arms toward Luke, and two more large stones launched away from the structure.

Luke dodged both stones with ease and they smashed into the wall behind him. Remembering how he'd defeated her before, he said, "Keep it up, S'ybll, and you'll find yourself homeless again."

Enraged, S'ybll lifted yet another large stone. Following her gaze, Luke saw she was aiming for Andur. He leaped over to Andur and yanked him aside. A split second later, the stone crashed against the wall where Andur had been standing. Luke shoved the startled scout against the ground and said, "Stay here."

S'ybll lifted two stones at once. Luke ran, weaving away from Andur and then turning to sprint straight for S'ybll. Without breaking his stride, he activated his lightsaber and dragged its blade through the nearest column, and then the next. The brittle columns shattered and collapsed.

S'ybll turned fast, trying to redirect the stones at Luke. She failed, lost control, and both stones crashed to the ground. Luke chopped through three more columns and then leaped away from the structure. He rolled and came up standing, turning just in time to see the broken columns fall.

The columns crashed down on top of S'ybll.

Or was it another illusion? Keeping his eyes on the rubble, Luke said, "Andur and Glaennor! Stay where you are! S'ybll might still be —"

Before he could finish, he was tackled from behind and felt a jolt travel through his nervous system. It was S'ybll. He hadn't sensed her coming. As her pale, bony arms locked around his torso, his own arms flung out away from his body, and his lightsaber fell from his grasp.

"Remember my touch, Luke?" S'ybll said, squeezing him tight. "When I'm done with you, I'll be more powerful than ever!"

Luke groaned.

And then the cavern's ceiling exploded open. It was unexpected, taking Luke, S'ybll, and the two scouts by complete surprise. The power of the blast sent Luke and S'ybll tumbling across the floor. Stones rained down from above, leaving an immense gaping hole in the ceiling, exposing the sky above.

S'ybll gasped as Luke fell back on top of her, causing her to lose her grip on him. As he rolled away from her, he glanced up through the hole in the shattered ceiling and saw what had caused the explosion. It was his X-wing starfighter, which hovered above the newly formed hole. The X-wing's cockpit was empty, but the socket behind the cockpit was not.

Artoo?

And then, from his comlink, Luke heard R2-D2's excited beeps.

Luke realized that his comlink probably had been working all along, but that S'ybll had manipulated his mind so he couldn't hear it. He also realized that the astromech had disobeyed his command to leave Tarnoonga, assumed control of the X-wing, and homed in on his comlink to pinpoint his position. But before Luke could answer the plucky droid, S'ybll shifted on the floor beside him.

Luke spied his lightsaber lying near the rubble. Using the Force, he drew the weapon through the air, and it landed with a smack against the palm of his hand.

S'ybll shrieked behind him. Luke ignited his blade and turned quickly to defend himself.

He didn't realize that S'ybll was already lurching toward him. His lightsaber went straight through her chest. S'ybll's mouth fell open and she made a croaking noise.

Luke switched off his lightsaber.

Teetering on her spindly legs, S'ybll sneered at Luke and said, "I never did like you." Then the mind witch's eyes rolled up into her skull and she collapsed upon the cavern floor.

Luke could hear his X-wing's engines through the hole in the ceiling. He kept his eyes locked on S'ybll's decrepit corpse as he reached for his comlink. "Artoo-Detoo, do you read me?"

The astromech responded with an affirmative beep.

"Land the X-wing and get down here," Luke said. "I need you to look at something for me."

Luke called out to the scouts to make sure they were both all right. He didn't take his eyes off S'ybll's dead body until R2-D2 entered the cavern and arrived by his side. Only after the astromech droid confirmed that he also saw the mind witch dead on the floor did Luke breathe a sigh of relief.

CHAPTER SEVENTEEN

"S'ybll?" Han Solo said with disbelief. He looked at Chewbacca.

Chewbacca growled.

Returning his gaze to Luke, Han said, "The mind witch? But I thought she was dead."

"Our mistake," Luke said.

"*Our* mistake?" Han chuckled. "Speak for yourself, pal. Usually when I see some old hag's arm sticking out from under a big block of stone, I just assume she's not gonna get up and walk away."

Chewbacca agreed with a robust chortle.

Turning serious, Han added, "You're positive S'ybll's dead? For real?"

Luke nodded. "Artoo saw her body. Psychic powers don't work on droid photoreceptors."

They were standing on the ground beside the *Millennium Falcon*, which had landed on the same wide slab of rock that supported the Alliance scouts' old freighter and Luke's X-wing on Tarnoonga. R2-D2 was inside the freighter, helping Glaennor and Andur repair their damaged controls. The storm clouds Luke had seen earlier had since passed, and the ocean that surrounded the mountaintop island was remarkably calm.

"Sorry we didn't get here sooner," Han continued. "As soon as we lost contact with you, Chewie and I figured you might need a hand. We really stomped on it, got here as fast as we could."

Just then, R2-D2 moved down the freighter's landing ramp. Seeing the droid, Luke said, "Well, I *did* get a helping hand from a trigger-happy friend of ours. If Artoo hadn't taken control of the X-wing and come looking for me, I can only imagine how things might have turned out."

R2-D2 responded with a whooping series of beeps and whistles, and then Glaennor and Andur followed the astromech down the ramp. Looking at Luke, Glaennor said, "Our control console won't win a beauty contest, but we're almost good to go."

Andur said, "General Solo, can you spare a power coupling?"

"No problem," Han said. "Chewie?"

As Chewbacca left to help the scouts complete their repairs, R2-D2 came to a stop beside Luke and Han. Han said, "There's something I'm wondering, Luke. You don't have to tell me if you don't wanna."

"What is it?"

"Goldenrod told me you went to Tatooine. Said you were on some kind of personal business."

Luke sighed. "Threepio talks too much."

"You're tellin' me? I've been saying that for years."

Suddenly, R2-D2 beeped with excitement. He wobbled slightly on his legs as a panel slid back on his dome to release an extendible antenna.

"What is it, Artoo?" Luke said. "You're picking up a signal?"

R2-D2 beeped again, and then activated his built-in holoprojector. A moment later, he beamed a flickering hologram of Princess Leia onto the ground before Luke and Han.

"Luke!" Leia said. "Are you all right?" Her voice was broadcast via the astromech's audio transmitter.

"I'm fine," Luke said. He gestured to Han and added, "We're all fine."

"Well, that's a relief," Leia replied. "But I wish you had told me you were leaving Aridus,"

"I'm sorry," Luke said. "It's just that . . . Leia, I found out some information about our father, and I wanted to investigate, so I —"

"So you risked your life?" Leia interrupted. She shook her head. "Did it ever occur to you that your . . . your *quest* for knowledge might just get you killed? Why are you so determined to find out more? Why can't you just stop thinking about him?"

Keeping his voice calm, Luke said, "Because I'm not you, Leia. I'd rather try to have some understanding of who our father was than forget about him entirely."

Stunned by Luke's words, Leia's hologram jerked slightly.

Han shifted uneasily on his feet. His eyes flicked from Leia's hologram to Luke and then back to Leia again. Leia continued to hold Luke's gaze.

"Please, Leia," Luke continued. "Please just listen. I don't want to upset you. I know you'd rather not talk about this at all, but . . . I'm not trying to convince you to forgive our father. I'm only hoping to figure out how he became the man he was and how certain circumstances of his life might have affected his decisions. I can't learn from his mistakes if I don't know what they were. Can we at least agree that we're better prepared for the future if we know more about the past?"

Leia's hologram was motionless and silent just long enough to make Luke wonder if something were wrong with the transmission, but then she nodded and said, "Yes, I can agree with that. But we have other concerns right now. If we talk more about . . . our father, we'll talk when *I'm* ready. All right?"

Luke smiled at this. "Thank you, Leia."

"The fleet will be leaving Aridus shortly," Leia said. "We've located Moff Jarnek on Spirador, and we need to go over a plan to apprehend him. Artoo has the coordinates for our rendezvous. I'll see you there." She broke the connection and the hologram vanished.

Luke looked at R2-D2 and said, "Get the X-wing ready for launch, Artoo."

The astromech whistled and moved off, heading for the X-wing starfighter. As the droid left, Han stretched his arms, looked at Luke and said, "So, that 'personal business' on Tatooine? That was about your father?"

Luke nodded.

Han lifted his eyebrows. "Yeah? Which one? The Jedi or the Sith Lord?"

"Aw, give me a break, Han. If you're just going to joke about —"

"Hey, hey, take it easy, Luke," Han said, raising his hands. "I wasn't needling you, just wondering who you're talking about."

"Oh," Luke said. "Well, I was trying to find out about Anakin."

Han nodded. "See, that's all I was askin'. So . . . how'd it work out?"

Luke shrugged. "Not the way I expected." He turned his gaze to the ocean. "I learned from a HoloNet search that Anakin was on Tatooine when he was a boy. From what I gathered afterward, at least a few people considered him to be a remarkable person and even thought well of him. But his life was also a lot more complicated than I ever imagined. There's still so much I *don't* know about him." Still looking at the ocean, Luke said, "As much as I might ever learn about my father, I can't even begin to put myself in his shoes. I don't think I'll ever really know who he was."

"Yeah, that may be," Han said as he looked out over the ocean too. "But the way I see things, knowing who your father was isn't nearly as important as knowing who you are."

Luke looked at Han. "Say that again?"

"Naw," Han said. "You heard me the first time."

EPILOGUE

Imperial Moff Harlov Jarnek didn't think anyone could touch him, especially after he used the Star Destroyers under his command to blockade the planet Spirador, where he had a private palace.

He was resting in a lounge chair in the palace, watching a holovid, when he heard one of his servant droids walk into the room. Although Jarnek hadn't heard any alarms go off, he felt a sudden panic when he turned to look at the approaching droid.

The droid's chest had been equipped with concealed blasters to kill trespassers, but Jarnek could see clearly that the droid was no longer prepared to stop anyone, because its chest was gone, along with its head and arms. It looked as though some kind of industrial laser had cut the droid in half, just above the waist.

The droid's remains tripped and collapsed across the floor.

Jarnek couldn't imagine how anyone could have

made it through the blockade and infiltrated his palace. He had stormtroopers as well as droids monitoring the entire building. He jumped out of his chair and was about to run for a blaster that he kept on a nearby table when a hooded man appeared in the same doorway through which the damaged droid had entered. The hooded man said, "You're under arrest, Moff Jarnek."

Glaring at the intruder, Jarnek bellowed, "Who do you think you are?"

"I'm Luke Skywalker," Luke said as he pulled back his hood. "I'm a Jedi."

ACKNOWLEDGMENTS

In December of 1976, my brother Corey let me borrow his copy of *Star Wars*, a novelization, written by Alan Dean Foster, of the then-forthcoming movie. I can't deny that Ralph McQuarrie's cover art totally reeled me in. I am very grateful to these gentlemen for introducing me to the adventures of Luke Skywalker.

A New Hope: The Life of Luke Skywalker incorporates dialogue and situations from deleted scenes of writer/director George Lucas's film *Star Wars*: *Episode IV A New Hope* and transcribed dialogue from the *Star Wars* Radio Drama, by Brian Daley. It also incorporates plots and details from previously published stories, notably "Iceworld" and "The Paradise Detour" from the *Star Wars* comic, by Archie Goodwin and Al Williamson; the *Star Wars* comic book stories "Crucible," by Chris Claremont and Archie Goodwin, and "Luke Skywalker's Walkabout," by Phill Norwood; and the novel *Tatooine*

Ghost, by Troy Denning. I am indebted to all these writers.

My daughter Dorothy, who's increasingly the *Star Wars* expert in our house, gave me some very useful story ideas. Several friends at *Star Wars* Fanboy Association, including Jean-François Boivin, Joe Bongiorno, Rich Handley, Chaz LiBretto, James McFadden, Abel G. Peña, Josh Radke, and Dan Wallace, were extremely generous with their knowledge about Luke Skywalker's life and lightsabers.

My endless thanks to Annmarie Nye at Scholastic, and J. W. Rinzler and Leland Chee at Lucasfilm, for giving me the opportunity to revisit the worlds of *Star Wars*.

ABOUT THE AUTHOR

Ryder Windham's many books for Scholastic include *Star Wars: The Rise and Fall of Darth Vader*; *Star Wars: The Life and Legend of Obi-Wan Kenobi*; *Indiana Jones and the Pyramid of the Sorcerer*; junior novelizations of the *Star Wars* and *Indiana Jones* movies; and the nonfiction book *What You Don't Know About Animals*. He is also the author of *Star Wars: The Clone Wars — Secret Missions* (Penguin), *Star Wars: The Ultimate Visual Guide* (DK), and *You Know You're in Rhode Island When . . .* (Globe Pequot). With Pete Vilmur, he is the coauthor of *Star Wars: The Complete Vader* (Del Rey). He lives in Providence, Rhode Island, with his family.

There's more adventure in store for Luke in

R E B E L ⦿ F O R C E

BOOK #1: TARGET

Luke Skywalker tightened his grip on the lightsaber. Frozen in place, he held his breath, listening.

It was too dark to see, but he could sense *it* out there somewhere, watching him. *Playing* with him. And at any moment —

PING!

The shot screamed past. Luke backed up against a tree, then lashed out with the lightsaber. The blue blade whirled up and around in a smooth, glowing arc. But it sliced through empty air.

PING! PING!

His heart thudding, Luke whipped the lightsaber from side to side, struggling to block the blasts. He was always an instant too late. He took a deep breath and warned himself not to panic.

Use the Force, Luke. He could hear old Ben Kenobi

advising him, but of course it was only his imagination. Ben was dead. Still, Luke tried to feel the Force. Ben had said that he need only reach for it and it would be there.

Luke reached.

Nothing.

But then: a small click. Like a weapon being cocked. Luke lunged to his right, slashing down with the lightsaber in a single, fluid motion. More shots streaked past, and Luke spun around, sweeping the glowing saber from one side to the other, deflecting the spray.

Grinning, Luke raised the lightsaber over his head, ready to deflect the next barrage of fire. But instead of slicing through air, the weapon struck something solid. Luke tensed, then — realizing what was about to happen — leaped out of the way.

Too late — again.

The blow came to the back of his head. Luke dropped the lightsaber and went down, slamming hard into the overgrown jungle weeds. A heavy weight landed on top of him, pinning him down. His fingers scraped the ground, but came up with nothing but dirt.

A soft click, as his assailant readied his weapon.

"Nooo!" Luke screamed. "Don't —"

Direct hit.

"Ow!" Luke complained. It may have been just a sting burst, but a direct hit to the shoulder still *hurt*. He whipped off his blindfold and glared at R2-D2, who came rolling out from behind the tree, looking as pleased with himself as an astromech droid could look.

"Artoo, that's not fair!" Luke gestured at the tree branch pinning him flat on his back. "I couldn't block the shot like this, could I? You should have waited!"

R2-D2 released a trill of beeps and whistles.

Luke sighed. He'd spent enough time around the droid to guess what he was trying to say. "I know, I know. In a real fight, the enemy wouldn't wait for me to be ready." Not to mention that in a real fight, the enemy would be shooting a blaster, rather than sting bursts — and Luke would be dead.

"Come on, Artoo," he finally said. "Help me out here."

R2-D2 beeped again, but didn't move.

Luke sighed. The astromech droid may have been his most loyal companion, but he was also more than a little sensitive. "Okay, I'm sorry I said you weren't playing fair," he apologized.

The droid beeped happily and rolled toward Luke, nudging his lightsaber into his outstretched hand. Soon Luke had sliced away enough of the heavy bough to climb out from under it. He stood up and dusted off.

All around him, the lush green jungle rustled and chirped, alive with the calls of the many species native to Yavin 4. Luke couldn't help feeling like they were all laughing at him.

Better them than Han, he thought, switching off his lightsaber and sliding it back into the holster hanging at his waist. Luke knew Han meant well — still, Luke had decided it might be better to practice in the jungle, with no one to watch him but R2-D2. He'd need a lot more practice if he was ever going to be a Jedi Master like Ben Kenobi.

His comlink beeped, driving away the dark thoughts.

"Where are you, kid?" Han's familiar voice asked. "Leia's been looking everywhere for you."

Luke grinned, glad there was no one but R2-D2 and a few mucous salamanders around to see how pleased he was to hear that. Ever since he had rescued Leia Organa — okay, since he *and* Han had rescued her — from the Death Star, Luke had felt a special connection to the Alderaan princess. Unfortunately, Han seemed to feel one, too.

"Then why didn't *she* call me?" Luke asked.

"Guess Her Highness has better things to do," Han joked. "Or maybe she's just afraid to get too close when you're waving around that lightsaber."

Luke glared at R2-D2. "How did you know I — ?"

"Blame Threepio," Han said. "That bucket of bolts has a bigger mouth than a Whiphid."

"Well, tell Leia you found me, and I'm fine."

"Tell her yourself, kid," Han said. "General Dodonna's called some kind of top priority meeting back at Base One — and we're the guests of honor."